HAR... Presents

*Great news! From this month onward,
Harlequin Presents® is offering you more!*

Now, when you go to your local bookstore, you'll
find that you have *eight* Harlequin Presents® titles
to choose from—more of your favorite authors,
more of the stories you love.

To help you make your selection from our July
books, here are the fabulous titles that are available:
Prince of the Desert by Penny Jordan—hot desert
nights! *The Scorsolini Marriage Bargain* by
Lucy Monroe—the final part of an unforgettable
royal trilogy! *Naked in His Arms* by Sandra Marton—
the third Knight Brothers story and a sensationally
sensual read to boot! *The Secret Baby Revenge* by
Emma Darcy—a passionate Latin lover and a shocking
secret from his past! *At the Greek Tycoon's Bidding*
by Cathy Williams—an ordinary girl and the most
gorgeous Greek millionaire! *The Italian's Convenient
Wife* by Catherine Spencer—passion, tears and joy
as a marriage is announced! *The Jet-Set Seduction*
by Sandra Field—fasten your seat belt and prepare
to be whisked away to glamorous foreign locations!
Mistress on Demand by Maggie Cox—he's rich,
ruthless and really...irresistible!

Remember, in July, Harlequin Presents® promises
more reading pleasure. Enjoy!

Harlequin Presents®

UNCUT

Even more passion for your reading pleasure!

Escape into a world of intense passion and
scorching romance! You'll find the drama,
the emotion, the international settings and
happy endings that you've always loved in
Harlequin Presents® books. But we've turned
up the thermostat just a little, so that the
relationships really sizzle. Careful, they're
almost too hot to handle!

Look for some of your favorite bestselling
authors in Harlequin Presents®

UNCUT!

Coming Soon:

Love-Slave to the Sheikh
by Miranda Lee
(August)

Taken for His Pleasure
by Carol Marinelli
(September)

Sandra Marton

Naked in His Arms

uNcut

HARLEQUIN®

TORONTO • NEW YORK • LONDON
AMSTERDAM • PARIS • SYDNEY • HAMBURG
STOCKHOLM • ATHENS • TOKYO • MILAN • MADRID
PRAGUE • WARSAW • BUDAPEST • AUCKLAND

ISBN-13: 978-0-373-12549-4
ISBN-10:   0-373-12549-6

NAKED IN HIS ARMS

First North American Publication 2006.

Copyright © 2006 by Sandra Myles.

This edition published by arrangement with Harlequin Books S.A.

www.eHarlequin.com

Printed in U.S.A.

All about the author…
Sandra Marton

SANDRA MARTON wrote her first novel while she was still in elementary school. Her doting parents told her she'd be a writer someday and Sandra believed them. In high school and college, she wrote dark poetry nobody but her boyfriend understood, though looking back, she suspects he was just being kind. As a wife and mother, she wrote murky short stories in what little spare time she could manage, but not even her boyfriend-turned-husband could pretend to understand those. Sandra tried her hand at other things, among them teaching and serving on the board of education in her hometown, but the dream of becoming a writer was always in her heart.

At last Sandra realized she wanted to write books about what all women hope to find: love with that one special man; love that's rich with fire and passion; love that lasts forever. She wrote a novel, her very first, and sold it to the Harlequin Presents line. Since then, she's written more than sixty books, all of them featuring sexy, gorgeous, larger-than-life heroes. She's a four-time RITA® Award finalist. From *Romantic Times BOOKclub* she's received five awards for Best Harlequin Presents of the Year and a Career Achievement Award for Series Romance. Sandra lives with her very own sexy, gorgeous, larger-than-life hero in a sun-filled house on a quiet country lane in the northeastern United States.

PROLOGUE

HE WAS a hard-bodied, six foot four inches of angry male.

His hair was midnight-black, his eyes deep-sea green. He had the high cheekbones of his half-Comanche mother; the firm jaw of his Texas father.

Tonight, the elegant savagery of his mother's people ran hot in his blood.

He stood in a room where darkness was broken by ivory swaths of moonlight. Shadows lurked in the corners, lending an ominous chill to the air. The sighing of the wind through the trees outside the house added to the sense of disquiet.

The restless stirrings of the woman asleep in the big four-poster bed were a manifestation of it.

She was alone, this woman he'd thought he loved. This woman he knew. Knew, intimately.

The delicacy of her scent, a whisper of spring lilacs. The silky glide of her gold-streaked chestnut hair against his skin. The taste of her nipples, warm and sweet on his tongue.

His jaw tightened. Oh, yes. He knew her. At least, that was what he'd thought.

Long moments passed. The woman murmured in her

sleep and tossed her head uneasily. Was she dreaming of him? Of what a fool she'd made of him?

All the more reason to have come here tonight.

Closure. The glib catchall of overpaid twenty-first-century shrinks who didn't have the damnedest idea of what it really meant.

Alex did. And closure was what he'd have as he took the woman in this bed, one final time.

Took her, knowing what she was. Knowing that she had used him. That everything they'd shared had been a lie.

He would wake her from her dream. Strip her naked. Pin her hands high over her head and make sure she looked into his eyes as he took her so that she could see it meant nothing to him, that having sex with her was a physical release and nothing more.

There'd been dozens of women before her and there'd be dozens after her. Nothing about her, or what they'd done in each other's arms, was memorable.

He understood that.

Now, he needed to be sure she did, too.

Alex bent over the bed. Grasped the edge of the duvet that covered her and drew it aside.

She was wearing a nightgown. Silk, probably. She liked silk. So did he. He liked the feel of it under his fingers, the way it had slid over her skin all those times he'd made love to her with his body, his hands, his mouth.

He looked down at her. She was beautiful; there was no denying that. She had a magnificent body. Long. Ripe. Made for sex.

He could see the shape of her breasts through the thin silk. Rounded like apples, tipped with pale pink nipples so responsive that he knew he had only to bend his head

SANDRA MARTON 9

to her, let the tip of his tongue drift across the delicate flesh, breathe against it to draw a guttural moan of pleasure from her throat.

His gaze moved lower, to the shadow of her mons, a dark umbra visible through the silk gown. He remembered the softness of the curls there. The dark, honey-gold color. The little cries she'd made when he stroked her, parted her labia with the tips of his fingers, put his mouth against her, sought out the hidden bud that awaited him and licked it, drew it into his mouth as she arched toward him and sobbed his name.

Lies, all of it. No surprise. She was a woman who loved books and the fantasy world in them.

But he was a warrior, his very survival grounded in reality. How come he'd forgotten that?

How come his body was turning hard, just watching her? That he still wanted her enraged him.

He told himself it was normal. That it was simple biology. Part A fit into part B, and part A had a mind all its own.

Maybe. And maybe that was why he had to do this. One last encounter, especially in this bed. One last time to taste her. To bury himself deep between her silken thighs. Surely, that would burn the rage out of him.

Now, he thought, and he feathered his fingers lightly across her nipples.

"Cara."

His voice was strained. She whimpered in her sleep but she didn't awaken. He said her name again, touched her again, and her eyes flew open. He watched as they filled with terror.

Just before she could scream, he pulled off his black ski mask and let her see his face.

Her expression changed, went from terror to something he couldn't identify.

"Alex?" she whispered.

"Uh-huh. The proverbial bad penny, baby."

"But how…how did you get in?"

His smile was slow and chilling. "Did you really think a security system could keep me out?"

For the first time, she seemed to realize she was almost naked. Her face colored; she reached for the duvet but he shook his head.

"You're not going to need that."

"Alexander. I know you're angry…"

"Is that what you think I am?" His lips curved in a smile that used to strike fear in the hearts of those he'd dealt with in what he thought of as his other life. "Take off that nightgown."

"No! Alex, please! You can't—"

He bent and put his mouth against hers, kissing her savagely even as she struggled against him. Then he grasped the neckline of the flimsy nightgown and ripped it from her.

"You're wrong," he said. "I can do anything tonight, Cara. And I promise you, I will."

CHAPTER ONE

NOBODY had ever asked Alexander Knight if a man's belly could really knot with anxiety but if someone had, he'd have laughed and said bellies couldn't knot any more than pigs could fly.

Besides, why ask him?

Anxiety wasn't a word in his vocabulary.

He knew what it meant to feel his nerves tense, his blood pound. Taut anticipation, after all, had been part of his life for a long time. You couldn't put in years in Special Forces and then in covert ops without experiencing moments of stress, but that wasn't the same thing.

Why would a man be anxious when he'd trained himself to face danger?

Alex pulled his BMW into a parking slot behind the building he hadn't seen in three years. Hadn't seen, hadn't thought of....

Hell, that was a lie. There'd been too many dreams where he'd awakened, heart pounding, sheets tangled and sweaty.

The first thing he and his brothers had agreed on, even before they'd come up with the idea of starting a company called Risk Management Specialists, was that there wasn't a way in hell they'd ever walk through these smoked-glass doors again.

"Not me," Matt had said grimly.

"Or me," Cam had added.

And Alex had said, *Damned right.* It would be a hot day in January before he so much as drove by the freaking place.

His jaw tightened.

So much for promises. It was November in D.C., the weather gray and cold, and he was going through those damned doors, walking across the tiled floor to the security desk.

The hell of it was, it all felt as familiar as if he'd never left. He even found himself reaching into his pocket for his ID card but, of course, there was no card in his pocket, there was only the letter that had brought him here today.

He gave his name to the guard, who checked it first against a list on his clipboard, then on his computer monitor.

"Move forward, please, Mr. Knight."

Alex stepped into the seemingly benign embrace of the security gate.

Checkpoint one, he thought, as the electronic snoops did a preliminary scan. This was his last chance to turn and walk straight out the doors.

A second guard handed him a visitor's ID badge.

"Elevators are straight ahead, sir."

He knew where the damned elevators where. Knew, after he stepped inside and pressed the button, that it would take two seconds for the doors to slide shut, seven for the ride up to the sixteenth floor. Knew he'd step out into what looked like a corridor in any office building—except that the luminescent ceiling was filled with lasers and God only knew what else, all checking him from head to toe, and that the plain black door marked Authorized Entry Only would open after he touched his thumb to a keypad and looked straight ahead so that another laser could scan his retina and verify that he really was Alexander Knight, spook.

Ex-spook, Alex reminded himself. Still, he pressed his thumb to the pad, just to see what would happen. To his surprise, it activated the retinal scan and a couple of seconds later, the black door swung open exactly as it had years ago.

Nothing had changed, not even the woman wearing a dark gray suit seated behind the long desk facing the door. She rose to her feet as she had a hundred times in the past.

"The director's expecting you, Mr. Knight."

No "Hello." No "How have you been?" Just the same brusque greeting she'd always offered when he'd had to stop here between assignments.

Alex followed her down a long hall to another closed door. This one, however, opened at the turn of a knob, revealing a large office with bulletproof glass windows overlooking the Beltway that circled Washington.

The man at the cherrywood desk looked up, smiled and rose from his chair. He was the only change in this place. The old director who Alex had worked for was gone. His assistant had replaced him, his name was Shaw, and Alex had never liked him.

"Alex," Shaw said. "It's good to see you again."

"It's good to see you, too," Alex replied.

It was a lie, but lies were the lifeblood of the Agency.

"Sit down, please. Make yourself comfortable. Have you had breakfast? Would you like some coffee or tea?"

"Nothing, thank you."

The director sat back in his leather swivel chair and folded his hands over his slight paunch.

"Well, Alex. I hear you're doing quite well."

Alex nodded.

"That company of yours—Risk Management Specialists, is that the name? I hear excellent things about the work you and your brothers do." The director gave a just-between-us-boys chuckle. "Quite a compliment to us, I think. It's nice to know the techniques you learned here haven't gone to waste."

Alex's smile was tight. "Nothing we learned here has gone to waste. We'll always remember all of it."

"Will you?" the director said, and suddenly the phony smile was gone. He sat forward, folded his hands on his desk, his blue eyes boring into Alex's. "I hope so. I hope you remember the pledge you took when you joined the Agency. To honor, defend and serve your nation."

"To honor and defend," Alex said coldly. To hell with phony pleasantries. It was time to get down to basics. "Yes. I remember. Perhaps *you* remember that the Agency's interpretation of that pledge was the primary reason my brothers and I resigned."

"An attack of schoolboy conscience," the director said, just as coldly. "Misguided and misplaced."

"I heard this lecture before. You'll understand why I'm not interested in hearing it again. If that's why you asked me to come—"

"I asked you to come because I need you to serve your country again."

"No," Alex said, and rose to his feet.

"Damn it, Knight…" The director took a deep breath. "Sit down. At least listen to what I have to say."

Alex looked at the man who had been second-in-command here for more than two decades. After a moment, his face expressionless, he took his seat again.

"Thank you," the director said. Alex wondered how much it had cost him to say the two simple words. "We have a problem."

"*You* have a problem."

That garnered a sound that was almost a laugh.

"Please. Let's not play word games. Let me speak my piece in my own fashion."

Alex shrugged. He had nothing to lose because no matter what the director said, he'd be walking out the door and away from this place in another few minutes.

Shaw leaned forward. "The FBI's come to me because of a, uh, a delicate situation."

Alex's dark eyebrows rose. The FBI and the Agency didn't even acknowledge each other's existence. Not in public, not in Congress, not anywhere it mattered.

"The new head of the FBI is an old acquaintance and…well, as I say, a situation has arisen."

Silence. Alex swore to himself he wouldn't be the one to break it but curiosity got the best of him and curiosity, after all, didn't mean he'd get involved in whatever was happening here.

"What situation?"

The director cleared his throat. "The oath of secrecy you took when you joined us is still binding."

Alex's mouth twisted. "I'm aware of that."

"I hope so."

"Suggesting I'm not is an insult to my honor. Sir," Alex added, his tone making a mockery of the honorific.

"Damn it, Knight, let's drop the nonsense. You were one of our best operatives. Now, we need your help again."

"I already told you, I'm not interested."

"Have you heard of the Gennaro family?"

"Yes."

Everyone in law enforcement had. The Gennaro family was deep into drugs, prostitution and illegal gambling.

"And you know about the indictment against Anthony Gennaro?"

Alex nodded. A couple of months before, a federal prosecutor in Manhattan had announced the indictment of the head of the family on charges that ranged from murder to leaving the toilet seat up. If convicted, Tony Gennaro would live out his life in prison, and the family's power would be ended.

"The feds tell me they have an excellent case. Wiretaps. Computer files." The director paused. "But their ace in the hole is a witness."

"I don't see what this has to do with me."

"The witness has not been cooperative. After initially agreeing to help, the witness balked. Now the Justice Department is uncertain as to what will happen next. The witness has finally agreed to come forward—"

"Under pressure," Alex said, with a tight smile.

"The witness has agreed to come forward," the director said calmly, "but—"

"But, the Gennaros might get him first."

"Yes. Or the witness might decide against testifying."

"Again."

The director nodded. "Exactly."

"I still don't see—"

"The attorney general and I go back a long way, Alex. A very long way." The director hesitated. Alex had never seen him do that before; it made the hair on the back of his neck rise in anticipation of what would come next. "He feels that the usual methods of witness protection won't work in this particular situation. I agree."

"You mean, he's not eager to put this witness in a cheap hotel room in Manhattan, hit up his budget for a one-man guard detail 24/7, count on the hotel staff not to talk about their star guest or sell the info to the highest bidder?" Alex smiled thinly. "Maybe they've learned something while I've been away."

"What they need—what *we* need—is an experienced operative. A man who's been in the line of fire, who knows better than to trust anyone, who isn't afraid to do whatever it takes—*whatever* it takes—to keep this witness safe."

Alex stood up.

"You're right. That's exactly the kind of man you need, but it isn't going to be me."

The director rose, too. "I've given this a great deal of consideration. You're the right man, the only man, for this assignment."

"No."

"Damn it, Knight, you pledged your loyalty to your country!"

"What part of 'no' don't you understand, Shaw?" Nobody ever used the director's name. It hung in the air between them, a deliberate reminder of Alex's removal from the life he'd once led. "I'd say it was nice seeing you again," he said, reaching for the door, "but hell, why lie about it?"

"They'll never get a conviction without your help!"

Alex opened the door.

"They'll kill the witness! Do you want that on your conscience?"

Alex looked at the older man. "My conscience won't

even notice," he said tonelessly. "You should know that
better than any man alive."

"Knight! Knight, come back here—"

Alex slammed the door behind him and walked away.

He drove the BMW back to the airport, dropped it at the
rental place and bought a seat on the shuttle to New York.

Anything was better than another few hours spent
breathing the air in a town where politicians kissed babies
while the agencies they funded dealt in death plots
hatched by cold-eyed men who lived in the shadows.

He knew it was the same in every other government
across the planet, but that didn't make it easier to accept.

He had almost a full hour to kill, so he settled into
the first-class lounge. The attendant poured him a
double bourbon; the brunette sitting across from him
looked up from reading *Vanity Fair,* looked back down,
then did a double-take and looked up again.

Her smile would have made her dentist proud.

Somehow, the already short skirt of her Armani suit
slid up another couple of inches. That was fine with Alex.

The lady had great legs.

Come to think of it, she had great everything. When
she smiled a second time, he picked up his drink,
crossed the room and took the chair beside hers.

A little while later, he knew a lot about her. Actually
he knew all a man needed to know, including the fact
that she lived in Austin. Not too far from Dallas.

And she was definitely interested.

But even though he kept smiling, Alex suddenly
realized that he wasn't.

Maybe it was that session with the director. Maybe it
was being back in D.C. It had stirred up a lot of memories,

most of them unwanted, including what a young innocent he'd been when he'd taken the Agency oath.

Nobody had told him that words like "serve" and "honor" could be perverted into something that stole a man's soul.

His obligation to the Agency had ended the day he'd resigned. Besides, from what Shaw had said, this didn't have a damned thing to do with defending and serving his country.

It had to do with a crime family and a witness.

A witness whose life was in danger.

The brunette leaned closer, said something and smiled. Alex didn't hear a word of it, but he smiled back.

Shaw wasn't given to hyperbole. He used words like those only when he meant them.

Damn it, he should have listened to Matt and Cam. They'd had dinner together at their father's home. Things had changed in their relationship with the old man. It wasn't perfect but it was a lot better than when they'd been growing up. All it had taken to accomplish that, Alex thought wryly, was Cam almost dying and Matt involved in a shoot-out.

His sisters-in-law had bustled off to the kitchen to get coffee and dessert. He and his brothers had joked around for a while, even the old man joining in, and then Alex had casually mentioned that the director had asked to see him.

"He wants me to fly down tomorrow."

Matt laughed. "He must be nuts, thinking you'd come."

"You told him what he could do with his request, right?" Cam said.

Alex hesitated. "I have to admit, I'm curious."

"To hell with curiosity," Matt said bluntly. "Whatever Shaw wants, you can bet your ass it isn't good."

Later, his father had drawn him aside. He'd been quiet through the conversation, so quiet Alex had almost forgotten he was there.

"You never talk about your time in the Agency," Avery said quietly, "which makes me suspect it wasn't all pleasant. But you must have believed in it once, son, or you'd never have taken the oath that made you part of it."

It was true. He *had* believed. In the oath to serve and respect his nation, its people…

Damn it. A pledge was a pledge.

He was on his feet before he remembered the brunette. Hell. He'd completely tuned her out. The fixed smile on her face made him wince.

"Sorry," he said, and cleared his throat. "I, ah, I've changed my plans. I'll be staying in D.C. Business, you know?"

She looked surprised but she made a quick recovery, dug in her purse and handed him a small vellum card.

"Well, call me," she said brightly. "When you have the chance."

He smiled, said all the right things. But he knew he wouldn't call and, he was sure, so did she.

He parked in the same lot. Went through the same smoked-glass doors, through the same security gate. Rode up in the same elevator. Pressed his thumb against the same keypad, had his eye scanned by the same impersonal machine.

If Shaw's secretary was surprised to see him, she didn't show it.

"Take a seat, Mr. Knight," she said, and scurried down the hall.

Seconds later, Alex stood inside the director's office. Shaw rose from behind his desk, smiling broadly, and held out his hand. Alex pointedly looked at it, then ignored it.

"Let's get something straight," he said coldly. "I do this one thing, you never contact me again."

Shaw nodded.

"I work alone."

"I know you'd prefer that, but—"

"I work alone," Alex said sharply, "or I don't work at all."

Shaw's mouth thinned but he didn't protest.

"And I have *carte blanche*. I'll do whatever it takes to safeguard this witness without interference or second-guessing from you or anybody else."

Shaw nodded again. "Done."

"Tell me the basics."

"The witness lives in New York City."

"Married? Single? How old is he?"

"Single. Mid-twenties. And it's a 'she,' not a 'he.'"

A woman. That only complicated things. Women were invariably more difficult to handle. They were emotional, hormonal...

"The witness's connection to the Gennaros?"

Shaw's lips curved in a cold smile. "She was Anthony Gennaro's mistress."

No wonder she was important to the feds. And hostile. This particular lady would know a lot, including just how vicious Tony Gennaro could be.

The director handed Alex a large manila envelope. "That's everything we have."

Alex opened the folder and took out a photo. Gennaro had good taste in women. Excellent taste.

"Her name is Cara Prescott," Shaw said. "She lived with Gennaro until recently." He smiled coldly. "She worked for him."

Alex turned the photo over. All the details were there. Name, DOB, last known address. Hair: brown. Eyes: brown. And yet, the photo told him the words were meaningless.

Cara Prescott's hair would be the color of ripe chestnuts; her eyes would be flecked with gold, and her mouth would be a tender pink.

She had a look that could only be called delicate, even fragile. He knew it was only that, a look, but scum like Gennaro would have been drawn to it like the proverbial moth to the flame.

He looked up. Shaw was watching him with a little smile on his thin lips.

"Beautiful woman, don't you think?"

"You said she was Gennaro's mistress," Alex said, ignoring the question. "Now you say she worked for him. Which is it?"

"Both." The little smile twisted. "Then Gennaro took a more personal interest in her."

"And now she's going to testify against him?" Alex glanced at the photo again. "Why?"

"Because it's her civic duty."

"Can the crap, Shaw. Why has she agreed to testify?"

The director plucked a bit of lint from his dark gray suit coat. "Perhaps the thought of prison doesn't appeal to the lady."

"Federal prison isn't a day in the park but it's a hell of a lot safer than turning against the Gennaro family."

Shaw was still smiling, but his eyes were icy. "Perhaps someone told her she might not go to a federal prison. That New York might charge her with a felony, unless she cooperates."

"Did she commit a felony?"

"Anything is possible, Alex. Surely you know that."

Yes. Oh, yes. He did. And, the truth was, it didn't matter. In the dark world of the Agency, the end always justified the means.

"What else?"

For the first time, the director looked uncomfortable. "I may have understated her hostility."

"Meaning?"

"She's not just a hostile witness, she's hostile to accepting the government's protection. She may, ah, she may object."

Alex narrowed his eyes. "And if she does?"

"If she does, your job is to change her mind. Any way you see fit. Do you understand?"

Now Alex knew why the Agency had been called in. The feds wouldn't do anything that smacked of subterfuge or, even worse, coercion.

The Agency would. *He* would. Even now, doing things that danced on the edge of the law was Risk Management Specialists' bread and butter.

"Well," Shaw said briskly, "now to the details. You're flying the noon shuttle to New York. There'll be a car waiting in your name at Hertz, and a reservation at the Marriott on—"

"Tell your secretary I won't be needing any of that."

"I don't think you understand, Knight. This is our operation."

"I don't think *you* understand, Shaw." Alex took a step forward, until the men were only inches apart. "I'll run this my way. I don't want anything from you or this office, not until and if I ask for it. You got that?"

There was a long silence. Then the director nodded.

"Yes," he said stiffly. "I understand perfectly."

For the first time, Alex smiled. "Good."

Then he turned on his heel and walked out.

CHAPTER TWO

BY THE time the shuttle landed at LaGuardia, Alex had come up with a plan.

Before he made any kind of move on Cara Prescott, he wanted to check her out. The drab bureaucratese of the file Shaw had handed him didn't give him a feel for the woman.

He wanted to see Tony G's former mistress with his own eyes. Find out how she spent her time. Walk around in her space.

Then, only then, he'd decide what to do next.

Until recently, the lady had lived in Gennaro's sprawling mansion on Long Island's North Shore.

Now, she lived in a loft in lower Manhattan, one of those neighborhoods identified not by a name but by an acronym nobody understood. Shaw said the feds had found her without any sweat. They'd been surveilling her, he said, but he'd seen to it they were pulled off.

At least, that was what he claimed.

Another reason to take his time and check things out, Alex thought as he headed for a car-rental counter. He'd said he wanted no interference on this job and he meant it.

When he was ready, not before, he'd introduce himself to the Prescott woman.

"Introducing himself" was probably a nice way of putting it, he thought as he handed the rental clerk his charge card. Assuming the lady was as hostile as Shaw said, it wouldn't be a very polite meeting, but he'd worry about that when the time came.

He drove away from LaGuardia in a nondescript black minivan. Stopped at a mall and bought a black leather jacket, a black T-shirt, black sneakers and black jeans. He already had his cell phone with him. Then he went into a camping-goods store and added a gym bag, a flashlight, a thermos, binoculars, a nightscope and a palm-sized digital camera.

You never knew when gadgets like those would come in handy.

He checked into a big, impersonal hotel, put on the black clothes, packed the gear in the gym bag and made a phone call.

Within the hour, an old friend who asked no questions provided him with a loaded 9mm pistol and an extra clip. He shoved the pistol into the small of his back and the full clip into his sock.

He was as ready as he'd ever be.

By midnight, he was parked across from Prescott's apartment building. It was on a street Manhattan realtors loved, a commercial slum just waiting to turn into a yuppie haven.

No self-respecting New Yorker was going to pay attention to a black minivan, or to him.

He watched the building all night. Nobody went in or out. At five in the morning, he set his internal alarm for half an hour's sleep. A week spent with his mother's elderly uncle, a guy Anglos erroneously referred to as a medicine man, had taught him how to go deep inside himself to gain needed rest for his mind and his body.

At five-thirty, he awoke refreshed and finished the coffee in his thermos.

At eight, Cara Prescott came down the steps.

She wore a long black raincoat that flapped around her ankles, a newsboy cap that covered her hair and oversized dark glasses despite the grayness of the morning. Jeans and sneakers peeped from under the coat's hem.

Along with the phony name on the mailbox in the lobby—C. Smith—and an unlisted phone number it had taken him all of an hour to get, he figured this was her attempt at a disguise.

Anybody determined to locate her would see through it in a New York minute.

Either she believed in hiding in plain sight, or she believed in luck.

Alex watched her walk up the street. He gave her a head start. Then he got out of the van and fell in half a block behind her.

She made a stop at the Korean deli on the corner, came out with a foam cup of what he figured was coffee in one hand and a small paper bag in the other. When she headed back toward him, he melted into a doorway, waited until she went by, then fell in behind her again.

She went into her apartment building. He got into the van.

The hours crawled by. What the hell was she doing up there? If she spent her time locked away like that, wouldn't she go stir-crazy?

At four-thirty, he had his answer.

Cara Prescott came down the steps again, wearing the same long raincoat, the cap, the dark glasses even though, by now, the sky was charcoal. But no jeans peeped out from the coat's hem and the sneakers had given way to low-heeled black shoes. She walked briskly toward the corner, checked the traffic light, crossed the street and kept going.

Alex followed.

Twenty minutes later, she opened the door to a bookshop. A stooped-shouldered old guy with white hair greeted her. She smiled, took off the coat and hat and dark glasses…

Alex caught his breath.

She was demurely dressed. Dark sweater, dark skirt with an unexciting hem length, those practical shoes.

He already knew the lady had the face of a Madonna. Now, he knew she had the body of a courtesan. Not even drab colors could conceal her high, full breasts; her slender waist and gently rounded hips. She had long legs that he could almost feel wrapping around his waist. Her hair, a mass of gold-tipped chestnut curls clipped into submission at the nape of her neck, was sinful temptation all by itself.

A man could undo that clip, plunge his hands into those curls as he lifted that perfect face to his.

Alex's body responded in a heartbeat.

Tony G might be a stone-cold killer, but the son of a bitch had excellent taste when it came to women.

The old guy said something to Cara Prescott. She nodded, went to the cash register and opened it. That sight was almost as startling as the sight of all those feminine curves.

Gennaro's former mistress worked in a bookstore?

Either she was desperate for a job, or she had more brains than he'd credited her for. Her former lover would never think to look for his woman in a place like this.

Alex checked his watch. It was a little after five. The store's hours were on the door. It was open until nine in the evening. Excellent. It gave him a four-hour window, more than enough to get into her apartment.

Once he'd done that, he'd have a better handle on Cara Prescott. All he knew now was that she was hot looking, smart enough to try to lose herself in the city but stupid enough, greedy enough, to have gotten into bed with a man who ordered people killed without compunction.

He had to know more if he was going to come up with an approach that might land him her cooperation or, failing that, her compliance.

Getting into her apartment was child's play. A credit card slipped between the jamb and the lock did the job.

His estimation of the Prescott woman's street-smarts went down a notch, then zoomed up again when bells went off over his head.

Literally.

She'd tacked a strip of them right over the door.

Alex grabbed the bells, silenced them and waited. Nothing happened. Evidently, whoever else occupied the building had learned the primary New York rule of survival.

If something went bump in the night and you weren't the one being bumped, you ignored it.

He shut the door carefully. The lady might have other booby traps around. He waited again, until his eyes adjusted to the gloom. Then he took out his flashlight, turned it on and swept the area with its narrow beam.

The apartment was one enormous room. No walls, just yawning space filled with shadows. There was a minuscule kitchen and bathroom at one end, a stack of cardboard boxes at the other. Whatever else he'd expected of a woman who slept with a killer—gilt, fringe, cherubs—wasn't there.

So much for that stereotype.

There was no furniture to speak of, either, just a narrow bed, a chest, a couple of small tables and chairs that might have come from the Salvation Army.

He made his way through the place slowly, opening drawers and carefully poking inside without disturbing the contents. He found only the stuff most women had: sweaters, jeans, lingerie.

Lace lingerie. Bras that would cup her breasts like an offering. Panties that would ride high on her long legs and dip low enough so they barely covered what he knew would be gold-tipped, feminine curls.

Alex shifted his weight. He had an instant erection, one that strained at the taut denim of his jeans. He hadn't been with a woman for a while. Was he that desperate that handling this one's lingerie, thinking about how it would look on her, was enough to give him a hard-on?

Any man with enough money could have Cara Prescott. A woman had the right to do what she wanted with her body but if she chose to auction it to the highest bidder, she wasn't a woman he'd want in his bed.

He wandered into the bathroom. The sink was chipped and stained; an equally battered shelf above it held small vials and bottles. He opened one at random and brought it to his nose. Lilacs? He wasn't up on flowers or on perfume: he liked a woman to smell like a woman, especially when she was aroused and eager for his possession, but as perfumes went, this wasn't bad.

A narrow closet was crammed between the bathroom and the kitchen. He opened it, poked through a sparse lineup of drab skirts, sweaters and dresses. Half a dozen pairs of shoes were stacked neatly on the floor: this morning's sneakers, sensible heels. Not a pair of stilettos in sight.

Too bad.

The lady's endless legs would look sexy as hell in strappy sandals with heels high enough to give a nosebleed to the lucky man she wore them for. Heels, one of those lace bras, a pair of the matching panties, and her chestnut hair wild and curling over her shoulders would—would—

Alex scowled as he shut the closet door. This was pathetic. Who gave a damn what she'd look like dressed in next to nothing? Nobody but her lover, her ex-lover, and whatever attracted Tony G would never attract—

Click.

Alex froze.

Someone had just turned a key in the front-door lock.

He switched off the flashlight and looked around for a place to hide. The closet was it. It was deep, even if it was narrow as a coffin. Besides, he didn't have a hell of a lot of choice.

Quickly, he stepped inside, pulled the door toward him but didn't quite shut it. He slipped the gun from the small of his back and held it down against his thigh.

The front door swung open; the jingle of Cara Prescott's improvised security alarm told him he had company.

The lady of the house was at work. The feds had been called off. There were only two possibilities.

His guest was either a very unlucky burglar…

Or a killer on Tony Gennaro's payroll.

Each time Cara opened the door lock, she thought what a pitiful excuse for a lock it was.

She'd asked the super to change it and he'd scratched his head and nodded and said uh-huh, sure, yeah, he would.

So far, nothing had happened.

Okay. She'd deal with it herself. Tomorrow, first thing. Tomorrow was her day off. Too bad it was too late to call a locksmith now, when she had unexpected time on her hands.

Half an hour ago, Mr. Levine got a phone call. His sister was ill; he had to go to New Jersey. Cara had offered to keep the shop open but he'd said no, he appreciated it but she was too new, she didn't know enough about his system.

Cara smiled wryly as she locked the door from the inside.

She knew enough to know the old man didn't have a system. Not that she'd told him that. He'd been kind to her, hiring her despite her admitting she'd never sold anything in her life.

Even now, worried about his sister, he'd taken the time to assure her that he wouldn't hold back her pay.

"It's not your fault you won't put in a full evening, Ms. Smith," he'd said. "Don't you worry about a thing."

For one awful second, she'd almost said, "Who?" She still wasn't accustomed to being Carol Smith. Hair clipped back, no makeup, just a young woman on her own in the Big Apple.

Truth was, she'd never even known anyone named Smith. She had the feeling Mr. Levine suspected that. He'd asked for her social security card, she'd promised to bring it in but she hadn't, and he'd never mentioned it again.

"I have a daughter just about your age," he'd said when he'd hired her. "She lives in England and I like to think people look out for her there."

In other words, he was an old man, lonely for his daughter, and she was capitalizing on it.

But she wasn't going to think about that. She was doing what she had to do, to survive.

Anthony Gennaro wanted her to come back to him. The FBI wanted her to go into protective custody.

All Cara wanted was for her life to return to normal.

That meant never seeing Gennaro again and not testifying against him, either. No matter what he was, he hadn't done her any harm. Not the kind of harm that counted, anyway.

Besides, as she'd told the agents who'd interviewed her right after she'd moved out of his mansion, she didn't know anything.

You do, they'd said, *you're just not aware of what it is. That's why we want to take you into custody. We can keep you safe while we help you remember.*

When she'd refused, they'd gotten angry. Told her Gennaro would never stop searching for her. Made threats about sending her to prison.

That was when she'd decided to disappear from the Long Island motel where she'd spent a couple of nights. And how better to disappear than to move to

Manhattan, where you could lose yourself in the crush of humanity?

She found a job and a place to live and until she exhausted the money she'd saved during the months she'd spent cataloging the library in the Gennaro mansion, she was safe.

More or less.

Cara carried one of the kitchen chairs to the door and propped it beneath the knob. That and the old sleigh bells she'd found in an antique shop on Ninth Avenue weren't much of an alarm system but right now, they were all she had. She'd get the lock changed tomorrow but there'd still be the skylight….

She didn't want to think what it might cost to alarm the skylight.

"Look up there, Ms. Smith," the rental agent had bubbled. "See? You have a real skylight."

What she had was a way for somebody to get in from the roof, but there was no point in being paranoid. The FBI wanted her to believe Anthony Gennaro would hurt her, but she knew better.

He wanted her back alive, not dead.

Besides, skylight or no skylight, the rent was right. So she'd said yes, she'd take the big, ugly loft.

And here she was.

As for the skylight…she'd ask the locksmith for suggestions. He could gate it off. Make it impenetrable. Yes, and turn this big, empty space into a prison.

Good practice, considering that she'd probably end up there anyway, according to those two FBI agents.

Cara swallowed hard.

"Stop it," she said in a no-nonsense voice.

She wasn't going to give in to self-pity. What she *was*

going to do was take a long, hot shower, heat a can of soup and read a book until she was too tired to do anything besides tumble into bed and sleep.

Briskly, she slid out of her raincoat. Took off the newsboy cap and the dark glasses. Her sweater and skirt. Then she toed off her shoes and padded toward the far end of the loft, pausing in front of the closet, hand curved around the knob before she remembered her robe was on the hook behind the bathroom door.

The bathroom was small and badly lit. Its saving grace was a glass shower stall with top and side sprays and an abundance of deliciously hot water.

Cara switched on the light, took the clip from her hair, then opened the stall door and turned the shower on. Steam began rising, clouding the pebbled glass as she undressed and placed her clothes neatly on the closed—

What was that?

Her heart banged into her throat. Something was moving. She could hear it. A scuffling sound. Feet?

Was somebody breaking in? Was the FBI right? Would Gennaro send his men after her?

A little gray mouse darted from under the sink, shot across the floor and disappeared out the door.

Cara gave a weak laugh. A mouse. A mouse! Her imagination had turned it into a monster. She was letting fear dominate every aspect of her life.

No more.

Still…she felt a chill shrivel her flesh. For a moment, for a heartbeat, she'd been certain someone was here.

Watching. Waiting…

Ridiculous!

Cara stepped into the shower stall and shut the door,

lifting her face to the spray. The water and the steam would do their magic and ease away her fear.

She hadn't come this far to fall apart. Survival was all that mattered now.

Resolutely, she took a tube of shampoo from the shower ledge, squeezed some into her palm and began washing her hair.

CHAPTER THREE

ALEX didn't take a real breath until he heard the thud of the shower door closing.

Jesus, that was close!

His plan had been to get a handle on Tony G's mistress. He sure as hell hadn't intended to hold out his hand, introduce himself and say, "Yeah, you're right. I just broke into your apartment."

He'd make his approach in a public place. The bookshop. The deli. She'd be less likely to make a scene if there were other people around.

Women were like that. Innately passive. It was their weakness. He'd seen instructors work like hell to drum politeness out of them.

You don't like the way somebody looks, they'd say, *you scream, yell, make a scene. Make noise. Lots of it.*

Women in the program eventually caught on. Civilians rarely did. Raised to be polite, they struggled with the idea of calling attention to themselves. It was bull, but it was how it was.

And it would work to his advantage.

The Prescott woman wouldn't make a fuss if he approached her the right way.

So, he'd stay with his plan. After all, nothing had changed. She hadn't seen him. He thought she would, when she'd paused at the closet, so close he could smell her scent.

Lilacs, definitely. Soft and feminine.

She'd looked that way, too. Soft. Feminine. And incredibly sexy, walking around just the way he'd imagined her, in a lace bra and panties the color of cream, the color rich against her golden skin. No stilettos but she was a turn-on without them.

All he'd had to do was slip from the closet...

The way he did now.

She'd left the bathroom door open. He glanced at the shower. The glass was pebbled, translucent but not transparent. He could see her outline through it.

See that her arms were raised, her breasts lifted, her body gracefully arched.

Alex scowled, dragged his gaze from the bathroom and made his way noiselessly toward the front door, then paused. At least he could check the phones for bugs. He had enough time for that.

Working silently, he took out a pocketknife, undid a couple of screws in the base of the first phone...and found a bug.

Damn.

He put the phone back together and moved to the second one. Another bug. As he put the screws back in, thunder rolled overhead, its roar as loud as a freight train.

Thunder, in November? he thought, looking up at the skylight just in time to see a bolt of lightning blaze across the sky. It illuminated a small object in the corner of the skylight.

Something was up there that sure as hell didn't belong.

Alex grabbed a chair, put it under the skylight and climbed up. No good. He was six foot four but even with the added height, the skylight remained tantalizingly out of reach.

He got down, checked the area again, eyes sliding past the broom in the corner, then returning to it.

Maybe.

He grabbed it, got back on the chair. Success! A couple of pokes and the thing he'd spotted came loose and clattered to the floor.

The sound was like a gunshot and he held his breath, listening for the Prescott babe to come running, but the shower was going full blast.

Alex scooped up the thing he'd dislodged.

It was a wireless camera. Incredibly small, barely the size of an oversized button, and it was recording everything that happened here.

Including his break-in?

One thing was certain. If there was one camera, there were others.

The woman he was supposed to protect was being watched. By Gennaro's hoods? If Gennaro knew where she was, why didn't he just come and get her? It could be the feds, but Shaw had promised to call them off.

To hell with trying to figure it out. Whoever was watching her could damned well have watched him for the past half hour, too.

For all he knew, they were on their way here right now.

Thunder raged overhead. Was the shower still running?

Noiselessly, he made his way to the bathroom. Yes, it was. Tendrils of steam curled from the opening over the stall.

Slowly, he moved inside the room, ready to spring if

Cara Prescott chose this moment to turn off the water and open the glass door. She'd panic at the sight of him. There was nothing he could do to prevent that, but he did intend to control it.

Her panic would be all the worse because she was naked. That wouldn't matter to him. Sex didn't enter into this. She was a job, that was all.

But her fear, coupled with the element of surprise, could work in his favor. The old rules still applied.

He took a couple of deep breaths to slow his heart-beat and oxygenate his blood. *Now*, he thought, and in one quick motion, he slid the shower door back.

Cara Prescott whirled toward him. Her face contorted with fear and she gave a scream that might have curdled the blood of a man who'd never inspired terror before.

As for her scream bringing the neighbors…it wouldn't. The bells had proved that. And then there was the sound of the shower and the thunder rumbling overhead.

Still, why take chances?

He stepped forward, put one foot into the stall and wrapped his arm around her neck, covered her mouth with his hand and pulled her back against him.

"Pay attention, Ms. Prescott. Do as you're told and— Damn it!"

She sank her teeth into the tender web of flesh between his thumb and his forefinger. He yanked his hand free and adjusted it so that it covered her nose as well as her mouth.

She reacted instantly, her body arching like a bow against the threat of imminent suffocation.

"Do that again," he said, his voice a warning growl, "and I'll be forced to retaliate. I repeat, Ms. Prescott. Do as I tell you and you'll be all right."

He had her on her toes now, her head tucked against his shoulder in an ugly parody of a lover's embrace. Water streamed down on them both and still she fought him, hands clamped around his wrist, using up whatever air was in her lungs in a desperate attempt to save her life.

Alex released the pressure, let her drag in a breath, then covered her nose and mouth again.

"Listen, damn it," he said, putting his lips to her ear. Her skin was cool and wet; a strand of hair fragrant with the scent of lilacs drifted across his mouth. "Behave yourself and I'll take my hand off your nose. Fight me, and I'll keep it right where it is until you pass out. Understand?" She didn't answer, but her struggles were growing frenzied. "Understand?" he repeated, the word a hard demand.

She gave a frantic nod.

"Good. Just remember. One sound, one false move, and I won't give you a second chance."

He moved his hand so it covered only her mouth but kept his arm right where he wanted it, hard around her throat. She was on tiptoe, off balance physically as well as emotionally, and that was the way he intended to keep her for a while.

Her nostrils flared as she gulped for air; the sound of her breathing was harsh. Her body trembled against his.

"Easy," he said softly. "Calm down, and listen."

She shuddered, but he could feel some of the rigidity easing from her body. When it did, he slackened the pressure of his encircling arm just enough to show her he was pleased with her response.

"I'm going to take my hand from your mouth. I don't want you to scream. I don't even want you to talk. Do this right, you'll be fine. Yell, bite, come at me—whatever you try, I'll stop you. And I promise, Ms. Prescott, you'll regret it. Understand?"

Her eyes widened; he knew his use of her name had finally registered.

"Understand?" he said again.

She gave a jerky nod. Alex waited a few seconds. As he'd hoped, a clap of thunder roared overhead. He took his hand from her mouth, half expecting her to scream despite his warning, but she didn't.

Good, he thought, and swung her toward him.

He told himself to remember that her nudity gave him a psychological advantage but that it meant nothing to him sexually.

Still, only a eunuch wouldn't have noticed that her skin was the color of rich cream. That her breasts were full and round, her nipples the soft shade of pink you might see within a delicate seashell.

And only a eunuch, or maybe a saint, wouldn't have wondered if her breasts would feel silken against the roughness of his palms, if her nipples would taste like honey on his tongue.

Her face, as white as paper, grew two patches of crimson under his scrutiny. Shaken, she put one arm across her breasts and the other over her loins in an instinctive, age-old female posture of defense.

A useless defense, had he chosen to force himself on her.

He didn't like that she'd think him capable of that. He was a lot of things, had been a lot of things in his time with the Agency, but he wasn't a rapist.

When he took a woman, he wanted her eager for his possession. For the hard thrust of his body, the demanding caress of his hands and mouth.

Yeah, but who gave a damn what Cara Prescott thought? Her fear would work to his advantage. Deliberately, he let his gaze move slowly down her body. Taking in the flat belly and patch of gold-tipped curls she tried to hide was just a way of reminding her that he held the power.

And, goddammit, if he was getting hard, it wasn't anything personal. Danger created an adrenaline rush. A natural high that far surpassed any drug.

Add a beautiful woman, a hint of sex, and you had one hell of a mix.

He understood all that. If only his body would get the message.

He was seconds away from being fully erect. Already, he could feel his engorged flesh pressing almost painfully against the denim of his fly.

His reaction infuriated him. He didn't like being out of control, not even for a heartbeat. That this woman, one step up from a whore, should exert sensual power over him made it even worse.

Concentrating on that did the trick. His erection went south and his brain came online.

Towels hung from a plastic rod near the sink. He grabbed one and thrust it at her.

"Cover yourself," he snapped.

Her hands shook as she clutched the towel to her wet body. It didn't hide much—he'd somehow plucked a hand towel from the rack, not a bath towel. Just as well. It was enough to let her feel a little less exposed but not enough to make him lose the psychological edge.

Her breasts, full and beaded with water, rose above the towel's skimpy folds.

"I'm not a burglar. And I don't work for your lover."

Still no response. The smell of her, soap and water, lilacs and woman, rose on the humid air.

"I don't want to hurt you. Do you understand?"

She didn't respond for what seemed a long time. Finally, she jerked her head in assent.

"Good." A muscle knotted in Alex's jaw. "Now, step out of the stall. Nice and slow. No quick moves."

She did as he'd ordered, her eyes never leaving his. He tried to do the same but it was impossible. The towel wasn't just small, by now it was soaked. It clung like a second skin, drawing even more attention to her wet, naked body, and to hell with eunuchs and saints.

Only a dead man wouldn't have let his gaze drift down those curves again.

No wonder Gennaro had wanted her, he thought, and forced his eyes back to her face.

"My name," he said softly, "is Alexander Knight."

He saw her throat move as she swallowed. "What— what do you want?"

Progress. At least she was talking. It was time to ease up.

"I want to help you."

She made a sound that would have been a laugh if she weren't so scared. He couldn't blame her.

"I know about you and Tony Gennaro."

The color in her face heightened but her voice was surprisingly steady. "Who?"

Alex's mouth twisted. He had to give the lady credit. She was stark naked and scared witless but she was starting to pull herself together. That was good—but he didn't want her thinking she could outsmart him.

Time to up the ante.

"Don't play games, Cara. I don't like them."

The use of her first name was supposed to remind her that he was in charge. It didn't. The pulse in her throat still leaped, her eyes still shone with fear, but something about her had changed.

She was starting to plot a way past him.

Slowly, almost imperceptibly, her chin lifted. "Give me my pajamas."

His eyebrows rose. "What?"

"My pajamas. My sweats. There, on top of the toilet. Give them to me."

She wasn't begging. She wasn't even asking. She was giving orders in an attempt to assert some control.

He understood that. It was what he'd have attempted, if the tables had been turned.

He also understood that there wasn't a way in hell he could let her get away with it. That she was smart and tougher than she looked only meant he had to make sure she understood that he was a lot tougher.

Alex reached out. Deliberately, eyes locked to hers, he cupped her buttocks and drew her against him. His erection was instantaneous. Good, he thought coldly, as he brought one hand around her and ran his knuckles lightly across the swell of her breasts.

The flicker of defiance he'd seen lighting her eyes gave way to naked terror.

"Maybe you didn't hear me, sweetheart. I told you not to play games." His mouth curved in a cold smile. "Or maybe you figure you're a tempting enough package to get away with this crap. Well, you're right about being tempting." He moved against her, just enough so she could feel the heavy weight of his arousal. "You're very tempting." His smile faded. "But I'm not interested."

The look on her face called him a liar.

"Okay," he said softly, almost agreeably, "you're right. Under other circumstances, I might be." The wet towel clung to her breasts; he reached out, cupped the warm, rounded flesh and told himself to ignore the quick pull of lust in his belly. "But these aren't other circumstances, and I'm not interested in buying what you sold old Tony."

"I don't—" Her voice quavered, then steadied. "I don't know any Tony."

"Yeah, you do. You're gonna have to trust me here, baby. If I worked for the man, you'd be dead by now…but only after I first had you on your back, with your legs spread."

He'd wanted to make her flinch and it worked. Good. This wasn't a time for subtlety. Besides, a woman who slept with a Mafia *don* wasn't a woman with delicate sensibilities.

He needed her to be obedient. If he felt a twinge of regret at the way she was trembling, it was only because he'd been a long time out of this business, not because she was so heart-stoppingly beautiful.

Hell, what did her beauty have to do with anything? The truth was, a woman who knew how to use her looks could be incredibly dangerous. You learned that fast in the cloak-and-dagger world.

Alex grabbed the sweats and gave them to her.

"Get dressed," he growled. "Then we'll talk."

Talk?

Cara bit back a crazed laugh.

A madman broke into your apartment, dragged you from the shower, looked at your naked body with eyes like lasers, touched your breasts, God, *touched* your breasts, and she was supposed to believe he wanted to talk?

She sank her teeth into her bottom lip to keep from screaming and pulled on the sweats, hunching over as best she could to keep him from seeing more than he already had.

The sweats were old and ratty and oversized. The "oversized" part was good. At least, she felt less vulnerable. Standing in front of a brutal stranger, naked, had put a lump of fear the size of a boulder in her belly.

It had to be a good sign, didn't it, that he'd decided to let her dress?

"Okay," he snapped. "If you have questions, ask them fast."

If she had questions? She really was going to laugh any minute now…or pass out at this madman's feet.

How come he didn't look like a madman? If she'd seen him on the street, she wouldn't have given him a second glance.

What a lie, Cara. You know damned well that you would.

What woman wouldn't look at a man like this? He was tall, well over six feet. His hair was an inky black. His eyes were the deep green of a northern sea, his cheekbones so high they were like slashes in his hard, handsome face.

And his body.

Long. Lean. Taut with muscle….

"Do you like what you see, baby?"

Her eyes flew to his. He was smiling, a knowing smile that made heat bloom in her cheeks.

"I want to be sure I know what you look like," she said coolly, despite the slamming of her heart against her ribs, "so I can give the police an accurate description."

"Ah, Cara," he said softly, "that's not very bright." His smile tilted, became something that chilled her to the marrow of her bones. "If I were here to—how shall I put this? To do you harm, your sad little threat would make me think twice about leaving you alive." His smile faded. "I asked you if you had questions. If you do, you're running out of time to ask them."

She swallowed hard in an attempt to bring saliva into her dry-as-cotton mouth.

"You said you don't work for—for this man you think I know. Then, who do you work for?"

"The government."

She took a step back. "I told the FBI I don't want anything to do with—"

She clamped her lips together, but it was too late. Another of those feral smiles spread over his lips.

"Now, isn't that interesting?" he said softly. "You don't know Tony G but you've been talking with the FBI."

What was that old saying? The best defense was a good offense. Ignoring what he'd just said was a start.

"If you work for the government, let me see some proof."

"Like what? A badge? A photo ID?" His smile twisted. "A letter from J. Edgar Hoover?"

"Hoover's dead."

"Yeah, and guys like me would be, too, if we went around carrying ID. You're just going to have to take my word for it. I don't work for the FBI. I'm with a government agency that doesn't advertise."

"You have no way to prove what you're telling me," she said, trying to keep her voice from shaking. "You just want me to trust you."

"You've got it."

"Trust you, how? What do you want of me?"

"Like I said, I'm here to help you. To protect you. To—"

He swung his head toward the open door. His body, all that lean, taut muscle, tensed. Cara's mind flashed on the nature programs she'd seen, and how a tiger about to leap on its prey suddenly seemed to turn into a statue.

Goose bumps rose on her arms. "What?"

He held up a hand for silence. Slowly, he reached under the black T-shirt that fit his muscled torso like a glove and slid his hand into the small of his back. As if by magic, a deadly looking gun appeared in his hand.

A whimper of terror rose in Cara's throat. He hauled her back against him.

"Someone's at the front door," he said softly.

"I don't believe you! I don't—"

He swung her to face him, cupping her jaw in one big, hard hand.

"Your apartment's bugged," he said in a harsh whisper. "You've been under camera surveillance and, goddammit, if you want to live through the next couple of minutes, you're going to have to do exactly as I tell you. Understood?"

She stared at him in disbelief. Why would she do anything this man said? Bugs? Cameras? And now he claimed he could hear someone at the door. But the shower was still running. All *she* could hear was water and an occasional roll of distant thunder from the dying storm.

"I don't believe you." Her voice trembled; she hated herself for it but she had never been so afraid in her life. "For all I know, you're a—a maniac who broke in here to kill me."

Something flashed in his eyes. Anger. Contempt. She couldn't read it, but she had no difficulty interpreting what he did next.

"Goddammit," he said roughly.

Thrusting his fingers into her hair, he tilted back her head and took her mouth in a passionate kiss.

She struggled. Cried out. Fought with every inch of her body, but he didn't let up, didn't ease the crushing pressure of his lips on hers until, with a little cry of distress or, God help her, an emotion she refused to examine more closely, she closed her eyes and opened her lips to his.

He took her mouth fully then, invading it with his tongue, taking the taste of her and making it his own until, at last, he drew back.

"Now," he said harshly, "are you going to do as I tell you?"

Cara stared into Alexander Knight's cold green eyes. Then she took a deep breath and said, "Yes."

CHAPTER FOUR

Yes was the only possible answer.

She was at the mercy of a man who might be a killer, trapped inside her bathroom with no way out unless she cooperated. That kiss just now…that kiss had been all about domination and power and she'd responded as necessity demanded.

That one instant when she'd felt the earth tilt under her feet was understandable. She was in shock, or as close to it as you could get and still stand upright.

His claim that somebody was at the front door was bogus, too. The more she thought about it, the more she was convinced nobody, not even he, could hear anything above the hiss of the shower.

Telling her there was someone trying to break in was his pathetic way of convincing her that he was a good guy.

Right. And she was Sleeping Beauty.

Cara knew that she needed time if she was going to escape. The only way to buy that time was to go along with what Alexander Knight—if that was really his name—wanted.

She raised her head and met his eyes.

"Yes," she said again, "I'll do what you say."

She would…until she saw a chance to get away. Then, she'd run like hell.

"Get behind me as soon as I start moving," he said. "Stay close, and keep quiet. Whoever's outside that door isn't going to stay outside much longer."

He sounded as if he really believed what he was telling her. Was it possible? Anything was possible this evening.

If there really was somebody there, what would he do?

She looked at the gun in his hand, the intensity in his eyes—remembered the intensity of his kiss—and decided that maybe she didn't want to know the answer.

"Now," he said in a rough whisper.

He hit the wall switch and plunged the room into darkness. The sudden lack of light, coupled with the sound of the shower, seemed like the set for a horror film.

Cara shuddered. She was so close to Alexander Knight that her body brushed his.

To her surprise, he reached back and touched her wrist. "Everything's going to be fine," he said softly.

She could only hope it was true.

He slipped into the hall with her on his heels. He might be the enemy, but at least he wasn't the unknown.

He moved soundlessly, flowing like a shadow through the yawning darkness. It occurred to her that he was dressed for this. His sneakers. His black leather jacket. The black T-shirt that clung to his muscled torso, the snug black jeans that hugged his long legs, were the clothes of a man who'd planned on remaining unseen.

Unseen, and silent. It was her bare feet that made the old floorboards sigh. She could hear the drumming of her heart, too, and the susurration of her breath.

If there *was* someone at the door, she was doing one fine job telling him they were coming, especially as the sound of the shower grew more distant.

Consciously, Cara slowed her breathing. Lifted each foot with care. Her eyes had grown accustomed to the dark and she saw that they were almost at the door, saw the chair she'd propped under the knob...

Saw the knob start to turn and, in the silence, heard the bolt start to slide back.

Snick-snick-snick.

Knight stopped moving and she stumbled against him. Without thinking, she wrapped her arms tightly around his waist. He turned, touched his hand gently to her cheek. Then he pushed her back against the wall and put his finger to his lips.

Don't move.

He mouthed the words rather than spoke them. She nodded.

Be careful, she wanted to say, *please, please, be careful*.

Abruptly, he exploded into action, wrenching the chair out from beneath the knob so that the door flew open. A man fell into the room. She couldn't see his face, only that he was big and he had an equally big gun in his hand.

"Looking for us?" Knight said pleasantly.

Then he raised his own weapon and brought it down against the intruder's skull in a vicious chop.

"Quickly," Knight said, grabbing Cara's hand as the man slumped to the floor.

"But—but what if you killed him?"

"No such luck. C'mon. Let's go."

Cara stared from the unconscious stranger to the conscious one who wanted to drag her into the night. What if the story he'd told her was upside down? What if the government had really sent someone to protect her, and now that someone was lying on the floor?

An old adage skittered through her head.

Out of the frying pan, into the fire.

"Damn it, Prescott, move! For all we know, he's got friends."

Cara gave up thinking and let herself be pulled into the hall and down the endless flights of stairs to the lobby. Her intruder—Intruder Number One, she thought, and knew she was rapidly approaching hysteria—shoved her unceremoniously into the corner.

"Wait here."

"But—but—"

He looked at her in a way that said he was going to kiss her again. She told herself she'd be prepared this time, that if he tried, she'd fight him. Told herself her heart was shuddering only in fight-or-flight anticipation.

She was wrong.

He bent his head, brushed his mouth over hers. Instead of fighting, she leaned into the kiss, lifted one hand and almost lay it against his cheek.

He was gone too fast for that to happen.

In an instant, he'd slipped out the door into the dark street. She heard a muffled cry. A thud. Then he was back, his hand wrapped hard around her wrist.

"Hurry."

"Hurry where? Was there another man?"

"No questions, remember?"

The street was deserted but she could see traffic at the corner intersection. Now. Now, she thought, now she could escape….

Add mind reading to her intruder's talents. He

cursed, scooped her into his arms and hurried to a van, opened the door and dumped her inside.

"Move over," he barked.

She did, scrambling over the console, banging her shin on the gearshift. He got in after her and jammed a key in the ignition. The engine roared and the vehicle shot forward into the night.

Cara told herself to stay calm.

She'd lost her chance to get away but there'd be another. Besides, maybe the man next to her wasn't crazy. Maybe he wasn't out to kill her. Maybe he really did work for some nameless government agency that wanted to protect her.

Maybe this was all a bad dream.

But dreams didn't involve your teeth chattering and your bare feet freezing. They didn't involve speeding through the Queens Midtown Tunnel and onto the Long Island Expressway with a stranger at your side, a man who'd broken into your home and hauled you, naked, into his arms; touched you with insolent arrogance…

Kissed you into submission.

A tremor shot through her. Her abductor—that's what he was now, wasn't he?—gave her a sharp look.

"Cold?"

"Would it matter if I were?"

Lights from an oncoming car slashed across his face. It was a hard face, all sharp angles and high cheekbones with a sensual, almost cruel-looking mouth. Those bones, that mouth, the unsmiling eyes gave him a primitive, strikingly savage look.

Savage, and beautiful. No question that he was the most beautiful man she'd ever seen.

A long-ago memory flashed into her mind, something whispered by a neighbor who'd sometimes taken care of her when she was little and her mother was at work.

Beware the devil, the woman had said in a Cajun lilt. *He walks among us in disguise.*

"Then, how will I know him?" five-year-old Cara had asked.

By his hideous face, the woman had answered. *Or by his beauty. Each of us sees the face we wish to see.*

Cara shuddered.

"Damn it," Knight said impatiently. "When I ask you a question, give me a straight answer." One arm at a time, his eyes never leaving the road, he shrugged out of his leather jacket and tossed it in her lap. "Put this on."

"I don't need it."

"Get pneumonia," he said sharply, "and you're no use to me. Put the jacket on."

At least she wasn't going to be killed right away. Cara sat forward and eased her arms into his jacket. The leather was soft; it smelled of night and rain and man.

This man.

Her throat constricted as she remembered him hauling her from the shower. The strength of his body against hers. The calculated stroke of his hand on her breast…

She swung toward him. "Who are you?"

"I told you my name."

"You know what I mean! Who sent you? Where are you taking me?"

He looked at her, a quick smile lifting a corner of his mouth.

"Twenty questions?" he said in a lazy voice that carried the faintest hint of a drawl.

"A thousand and twenty," she said, trying to keep her fear from showing. "But you can start with those."

"I already said that I work for a government agency you've never heard of. I'm taking you where I can keep you safe until the Gennaro trial."

"I'm not testifying. I already told that to the FBI."

"Argue that with them, not with me." He glanced in the mirror and switched lanes. "Look, if I'd wanted to hurt you, I'd have already done it."

It was a reasonable response. Unfortunately, nothing that had happened to her since the day Anthony Gennaro walked into her life was reasonable. Why would she start believing in reason now?

"And where is this place you think you can keep me safe?"

He swung the van onto a road lined with dark warehouses and parked trucks.

"You'll see soon enough."

It wasn't an answer designed to offer comfort, or maybe she'd seen too many movies about what happened at night at the ends of roads like this.

"This doesn't look very safe to me."

"It leads to a back entrance to Kennedy Airport."

"Do you think…? I am not getting on a plane with you!"

"Instead of arguing, how about looking out the rear window and telling me what you see?"

"For instance?"

"A car coming too fast. Or a car falling in behind us and staying there. Surprise us both. See if there isn't a modicum of intelligence lurking in your brain."

Then he shifted his weight, dug a cell phone from the back pocket of his jeans and flipped it open. Seconds later, he was deep in a series of one-sided conversations that all ended with the same word.

"Thanks."

"Thanks for what?" Cara demanded.

He didn't answer.

The road led to a police car that waited at a closed gate. A uniformed cop stood leaning against the car, arms folded over his chest.

Cara wrenched open the van's door and almost fell at his feet.

"Thank God! Officer! This man—"

Her mouth dropped open. The cop and her abductor were exchanging handshakes.

"This the suspect?" the cop asked.

"I'm not a suspect. I'm—"

"Yeah. I have to get her the hell out of the city, and fast."

"Officer!" Cara's voice rose. "I am not a suspect. I am his—"

"Well," Alexander Knight said, with a little smile, "she's that, too." He swept an arm around her. "Baby, don't say anything he doesn't want to hear, you know what I mean? You do that, you'll put him in a difficult position."

Both men chuckled.

"No," Cara pleaded. "Please, Officer, you have to listen—"

"Baby," Knight said, a hint of warning in his voice, and before she could say anything else, he swept her off her feet and kissed her.

The cop laughed. Cara gasped. Tried to cry out. Settled for sinking her teeth into her abductor's lip. He grunted, wrapped her hair around his hand and crushed her mouth under his.

Bite him now, she told herself desperately, bite him again, twice as hard as you just did….

And then his mouth gentled on hers. A slow wave of lassitude swept through her. She was exhausted, afraid, and yet the way he held her made her want to drop her head against his shoulder and let him do whatever he wanted.

"That's it," he whispered. "Stop fighting me. It'll be a lot easier."

She thought of the man lying inside her apartment, of the gun in the small of Alexander Knight's back…

And knew what he'd said was a promise and not an empty threat.

The police car led them to a small, sleek private jet, poised like a bird of prey on the tarmac.

The two men exchanged handshakes again. Then she was in her abductor's arms.

He carried her into the plane, gave a thumbs-up to the waiting pilot and deposited her in a leather seat in the cabin.

"Buckle up," he said briskly.

She didn't move. His mouth twisted; he reached for the seat belt and closed it around her.

"Remember what I said? Do as you're told, Ms. Prescott, and we'll get along just fine."

A sob of rage and despair rose in her throat. Without thinking, Cara slapped his face.

His head jerked back. For a moment, she thought he was going to slap her in return, but she didn't give a damn. She was tired of being treated as if she only existed to suit him.

He leaned closer and caught her chin in one big hand.

"You want to play games, baby?" he said in a rough whisper. "That's fine. We can play a lot of them when we get where we're going."

"I have the right to know where you're taking me."

"You don't have any rights unless I say you do." His smile glittered, though it never reached his eyes. "But I'll tell you anyway. We're going to a place I own. I'm not sure it'll be up to the elegant standards of your apartment but hey, what's that old saying about beggars and choosers?"

"You still haven't said where it is."

He stood straight. "Florida."

Was this his idea of a joke? Florida? More than a thousand miles from home? Another jolt of terror streaked through Cara's blood.

"Why?"

"Because it's safe."

"You can't—you can't do this!"

Another of those cold smiles. "Really?"

Desperately, she searched for a valid reason. "You have to file a flight plan. There are regulations. Security restrictions."

Alex raised an eyebrow. She was fast, he had to give her that. Scared as she was, she'd come up with a good answer. Good for anybody but someone like him.

"You're right," he said calmly. "There are all those things—but they're only incidentals."

The tip of her tongue—a pink, delicate tongue—swept over her bottom lip. Ten to one, she was about to come up with a change in tactics.

"Mr. Knight," she said, her tone almost impressively calm.

"Alex," he said, going along with it. "We're going to

be spending a lot of time together. We might as well be less formal."

"You say—you say you've been sent to protect me. Well, you've done that. Those two men…" She paused; he could almost hear the wheels turning. "You took care of them."

"And?"

"And, the threat to me is over."

"Is it?"

"You've done your job. There's no reason to go through with—with the rest of your plan."

He took his time answering. What response would serve him best right now? He knew damned well his passenger didn't believe he was one of the good guys. Hell, he couldn't blame her. On top of everything else he'd done tonight, he'd just told her he was going to fly her fifteen hundred miles from what she considered home, dressed in her sweats and his leather jacket.

Amazing how good she looked in that getup.

The sweats, visible under the open jacket, were oversized. They were also old, washed and worn until they had the thinness of silk.

He could see the outline of her breasts. His body clenched as he recalled the fullness of them in his cupped hands.

His gaze dropped lower, to where the thin cotton fabric hid a soft tangle of gold-tipped curls. Curls that he'd glimpsed when he'd taken her out of the shower, her body sleek and wet with water.

She was, without question, an incredibly beautiful woman.

Anthony Gennaro's woman. A thug who'd had her in his bed whenever he'd wanted her.

Now, Gennaro was trying to kill her.

How come she didn't want to believe that? She wasn't stupid; he knew that much already. Had she and Gennaro had a falling-out? Was she still hoping he'd take her back? It couldn't be much fun, living in a loft furnished with castoffs when you were accustomed to a North Shore mansion.

"Alex?"

His gaze swept up to hers.

"Please," she said softly, "listen to reason. I'm safe now. Won't you take me back to the city?"

Her voice trembled; her eyes glittered with unshed tears. Did she really think her performance would reach him?

His mouth thinned. She was wasting her time. She was a job he hadn't asked for, but he'd accepted it. Whether she liked him or hated him was unimportant.

"No," he said, snapping out the single word.

She sagged against the constraints of the seat belt.

"Why not?" Her voice rose; her careful control was at the breaking point. "Damn you, who's paying you? How much? I'll equal it. I'll double it! How much do you want?"

"Yeah," he said coldly. "I could tell from that place you live in that you've got a fortune." His lips drew back from his teeth. "Or are you offering me what you sold to Tony G?"

"Bastard! No-good, heartless bast—"

He leaned down and kissed her again, kissed her hard, ignored the way her hands rose and pushed at his shoulders, the way she tried to twist her mouth from his, kissed her until what had happened before happened again, until her whimpers of protest changed to whimpers of desire.

Her mouth opened to his. He allowed himself one long, deep taste before pulling back.

"Behave yourself, you'll be okay. Give me a hard time, and you'll regret it."

"I'll kill you," she whispered. "Do you hear me? Touch me again and I'll kill you!"

Alex took off his belt, wound it around one of her wrists and secured it to the armrest, took the safety belt from the next seat and used it to tie down her other wrist.

"Behave yourself and after we gain some altitude, I might untie you, let you take a pee, get a drink of water, whatever you need for the next four hours. Do we understand each other?"

She lifted her head. Looked into his eyes. And spat in his face.

His expression didn't change.

"You need to learn some manners, Ms. Prescott," he said evenly.

He bent down, took her mouth again, kissed her until she gave a little cry, the kind of cry his body hungered for. Then he walked to the cockpit, took the copilot's seat.

The jet's engines whined, the plane began moving forward.

Moments later, the lights of New York City were far below them.

CHAPTER FIVE

HE'D said he'd untie her once they gained some altitude, but an hour had gone by, they were high enough to play hide-and-seek with the moon, and her abductor was among the missing.

Cara gritted her teeth and tugged against the belts wrapped around her wrists, harder and harder until she was panting with effort.

With rage!

A snarl erupted from her throat.

How could this have happened to her? When everything had gone wrong, after she'd learned the truth about Anthony Gennaro, after the FBI had started bothering her, she'd run, yes, but she'd been careful. So very careful.

She'd taken a ramshackle apartment in the kind of neighborhood where nobody would think to look for her, a job that was an absolute guarantee of anonymity. She hadn't told anyone where she was going or what she was doing.

Cara turned her face to the window and stared into the blackness beyond the glass. She could feel her anger giving way to anguish and she couldn't afford to let that happen. Crying wouldn't change a thing. She had to deal with reality.

She'd never had a chance. Someone had been following her. Watching her. Listening to her, all along.

Just thinking about it made her feel sick to her stomach. Such awful violations of her privacy. Faceless men, watching her awake, asleep.

And now, she'd been abducted by a stranger.

A man who terrified her.

His voice reminded her of gravel and silk. His smile suggested he knew all her secrets…but he didn't.

There was no reason for him to know them. Not ever.

What frightened her the most was the way he touched her, as if he owned her. As if he could control her by putting his hands on her.

Images jumped into her mind. The way he'd taken her from the shower. The way he'd looked at her. The deliberate brush of his hand over her breasts and the feel of his body against hers.

Cara choked back a moan.

She understood what he was doing. That he was establishing his dominance. What she didn't understand was her own reaction to him. Her response to the stroke of his hand on her skin, the brush of his lips on hers.

He was everything she'd run from. A man who was stone-cold. Who lived by his own rules.

And yet—and yet…

Maybe she did understand it. She was emotionally wrung-out. Physically exhausted. All these weeks of living a nightmare had taken their toll. She was vulnerable, this man knew it, and he was using it to his advantage.

She had to stay strong and alert; she had to find her

abductor's weaknesses, capitalize on them so she could find the right moment to run.

But first, she thought, as exhaustion finally claimed her, but first she would close her eyes, just for a little while….

She was asleep.

Good, Alex thought. She was less trouble that way.

He started back to the cockpit, turned and looked at her again. Her face was pale; shadows lay like bruises beneath her eyes and her hair was a mass of shiny, tangled curls.

She'd had a rough night. One shock after another had taken their toll.

Right now, she looked like an ad for all the reasons a person shouldn't fly coach—except, she wasn't. A plane like this was first-class all the way. Big leather seats. Lots of elbow and leg room. Seat backs that reclined until you might as well be lying in your own bed…

Unless you were tied up. Couldn't shift around. Couldn't adjust your seat.

Like Cara.

Even as he watched, her head lolled to the side. Another couple of inches, she'd bump it against the window.

So what? His job was to see to it she made it to trial in one piece, not to worry about her comfort. She was alive, which was more than she'd be if he hadn't shown up. Why should he give a damn if she spent the next four hours trussed up like a turkey ready for the oven?

Her forehead bumped against the glass. She winced, murmured something unintelligible and jerked upright, but he knew it was a matter of time before the cycle started again.

Alex cursed softly, sat down next to her and quickly unbound her wrists. He slipped his arm around her shoulders to support her as he pressed the button that reclined her seat.

She sighed. Her head drooped against his shoulder; her tangled chestnut curls brushed silkily against his cheek. Another sigh, and he felt her warm breath on his throat.

He went still. Shut his eyes. Inhaled the fragrance of the woman in his arms. Then, carefully, he lay her back in her seat.

Cara shifted onto her side and drew her feet up under her.

He frowned. Her feet were bare. They were probably cold. *She* was probably cold, despite the fact that she was still wearing his jacket. He damned well was.

He watched her for a couple of minutes, a muscle knotting and unknotting in his jaw. Then he stood up, dimmed the overhead light, poked through a compartment, found a cashmere afghan and draped it over her.

There had to be another blanket….

There wasn't.

He sat down again, moved the seat arm between them out of the way, aligned his seat with hers and drew her against him. She came readily, her head settling against his shoulder, her body curving into his as if lying in his arms was something she'd done a hundred times before.

Alex swallowed hard. Stared up at the ceiling. Told himself it was okay because this way, she'd keep sleeping…

God, she was warm.

Soft.

So warm, so soft…

Sit up, he told himself sharply. *Sit up, move to another seat, do without a goddamned blanket. You've slept in a field in the middle of the freaking winter, with less on than you're wearing now….*

"Mmm," Cara sighed, and spread her hand over his heart.

Alex drew the cashmere afghan over them both. Twenty minutes. That was all he needed. Just twenty…

He awoke under attack.

Fists were pounding his chest. His shoulders.

Cara was trying to beat the crap out of him. He would have laughed, except she was getting in some good punches, so he grabbed her wrists, rolled her under him and pinned her down.

"Stop it!"

"You bastard! You thought you could take advantage of me!"

"I fell asleep." Damned right, he'd fallen asleep. What happened to that twenty-minute nap? "So did you. End of story."

"I wasn't asleep. I was dozing."

"I don't care if you were catching forty winks or playing Rip Van Winkle. You were sleeping, your head was bouncing around like a yo-yo, you were cold. I made the monumental error of untying you and covering you with a blanket. You want to turn that into something else, be my guest."

She was still struggling, trying to push him off her and, damn it, his body was having a predictable reaction to the thrust of her hips.

"Stop it," he growled, "or I won't be responsible for the consequences."

He moved against her, just to make sure she got the message. Her face turned red and she went still.

"Get off!"

"With pleasure."

He rolled away from her, got to his feet and ran his hands through his hair as casually as if nothing had happened.

God, Cara thought, how she despised him!

She sat up, glaring. "I have to pee."

She said it coldly, deliberately using the same words he'd used when they'd left New York. Did he think she wasn't tough enough for whatever game he was playing? That he could capitalize on the situation by making her feel helpless?

Although that wasn't how she'd felt, waking in his arms. For a moment, only a moment, she'd lain still, wrapped in the warmth of his body, comforted by his strength...

Cara felt the thick, sudden pulse of her blood and she shot to her feet.

"I said—"

"I heard you. The lavatory's in the back. Leave the door open."

"Excuse me?"

His eyes burned into hers. "The door stays open."

"That's out of the question."

"Your choice, baby. You want to go to the john, or not?"

God, he was so smug. So arrogant. She wanted to slug him but she knew he wouldn't let her get away with that a second time. Instead, she settled for fixing him with what she hoped was a look of utter contempt.

"I know what you're doing."

"Really." His lazy drawl set her teeth on edge.

"You're trying to intimidate me. Telling me I have no privacy, tying me to the seat... Nonsense, all of it."

His eyebrows rose. "Am I that obvious?"

He was laughing at her, damn it. That made her even angrier.

"Yes," she snapped, "you are."

"In that case," he said smoothly, "there's no problem with leaving the door open. As long as we both know the reason, why fight against it?"

Alex reached for her arm. She jerked away. He lifted his hands, stepped aside and let her move past him.

The view was better this way.

The sweats were baggy, but he had a good imagination and an even better memory. It was easy enough to recall the sweet curves of her backside and how silky her skin was there.

Going in, he'd known Cara Prescott was a stunning woman. Now, he had to admit she was also interesting.

And tough.

She was sure of herself, too. Sure she had him pegged right. He was a punk with nothing but muscle between his ears. That he'd tied her down to remind her he was in charge.

Well, yeah. But there was more to it than that.

He'd tied her because she had balls. He smiled. Or the female equivalent of them. The last thing he'd wanted was her storming into the cockpit and grabbing for the mike or the instrument panel. It wouldn't have meant a damn to the pilot, who was a Risk Management employee, but only a foolish man would let somebody mess around in the cockpit of a plane flying through the night at five hundred miles an hour.

Alex's smile faded.

She was a gorgeous piece of tail, she had courage and she was smart. She'd also warmed Tony Gennaro's bed.

Hey, it was a free country. A woman could sleep with whoever she wanted—he didn't have any hangups about sexual freedom for men and sexual innocence for women—but he had no interest in the leavings of a man like that.

Bottom line, his approach to her was strictly professional. Whatever he'd done—the kisses, the touches—had been, just as she'd figured, to keep her on edge.

Okay, so if she looked like a middle linebacker for the Dallas Cowboys, he'd have found other ways to keep her off balance, but one thing you learned in this business was to work with what you had.

And what he had was a woman who could turn a man on with a look, even when she was wearing sweats, when her face was bare of artifice, when, damn it, she looked as wholesome as somebody's sister.

For some crazy reason, that bothered him. Her looking like something she wasn't ticked him off enough so he clamped his hand on her shoulder and turned her toward him just as she reached the lavatory.

"What now?" she demanded.

"A body search, sweetheart."

"A body…?" Crimson striped her cheeks. "You are not going to search me!"

His smile glittered. "Want to bet?"

Her pupils widened, all but swallowing the hazel, green and gold of her irises. "But—but you know I'm not hiding anything. You saw me—you saw me—"

"Naked." His voice was rough. "Yeah. I did. But that was hours ago. Anything's possible since then."

It wasn't a lie, even if it wasn't the exact truth. He'd known prisoners who'd been searched and found clean to end up sticking a shiv into some poor bastard's gut a couple of hours later.

Okay. She wasn't his prisoner. Not really. And where could she have found a weapon since he'd taken her out of that shower?

The thing of it was, you played by the rules. The rules might be all that kept you alive.

He spun her around so she faced the bulkhead, caught her wrists and hoisted her arms over her head.

"Feet apart, baby."

But the rules had nothing to do with the feel of her skin as he slipped his hand under her sweatshirt and ran it lightly over her ribs. Ran it up further, to cup one breast and then the other. Feathered his thumb across her taut nipples.

Her breath caught. The sound was a sigh. A moan. A whisper that rocketed through him, turned his body hard as stone.

"Nothing there," he said in a voice that bore no resemblance to his own.

But that wasn't true. There was something there. The feel of her breasts in his hands. The swift tightening of her nipples. That little moan…

He ran his hand lower. Spread his palm over her belly. Her smooth, firm belly. Moved his hand lower again. Put it between her thighs.

Cupped her.

Heard the hiss of her breath.

Felt the softness of her curls. Felt— God, felt a sweet, sweet dampness against the heat of his fingers.

Alex groaned. Sweat beaded his forehead.

She was killing him.

And all he had to do for relief was push down her pants. Unzip his fly. Wrap an arm around her waist and pull her back against him, bury himself deep inside her, move inside her, feel her satin heat all along the length of his erect flesh.

The plane dipped, rose, then dipped again.

Cara stumbled back. He closed his eyes, ground his teeth together, let himself feel the softness of her against his swollen penis…

Goddammit, was he losing his mind?

"Okay," he said briskly. "You're clean." He reached past her, opened the door to the toilet. She didn't move. Didn't do anything. Then she turned and looked at him, her face white, her eyes enormous.

"How do you live with yourself?" she said in a thready whisper.

It was a good line. A terrific line. And it might have made him cringe if he hadn't heard her make that soft moan.

If he hadn't felt her feminine flesh weep delicately against his hand.

Could a woman fake that kind of stuff? Could *this* woman? He thought of her in Tony G's arms and knew the answer was almost surely yes.

"You said you need to use the john," he said brusquely. "I suggest you get to it."

Her mouth trembled. Oh, yes. She was good. Damned good, and trying to slide the door shut on his foot was a nice touch, too.

"Sorry, baby. Remember what I said? The door stays open." His lips curved in an insolent smile. "I'll be a perfect gentleman. Eyes on the ceiling at all times."

"You wouldn't know how to be a gentleman if your life depended on it!"

If looks could kill, Alex figured he'd be dead.

He put his foot in the doorway. She stepped back, grabbed the handle and yanked the door as far shut as possible.

The water in the sink went on. That made him laugh but, as he'd said he would, he turned his eyes to the ceiling and whistled softly through pursed lips.

Eventually, the door opened. She must have scrubbed her face because it shone like a polished apple. Her hair was wet and he figured she'd run damp fingers through it to tame it.

All she'd succeeded in doing was making it curl into dangling spirals around her temples.

"Better?" he said politely.

She shot him another look, more venomous than the last.

"You're despicable," she said coldly. "Did you know that?"

"A couple of people have mentioned it, yeah."

She swept past him. Alex followed, stood by while she settled into her seat and snapped on the safety belt.

Then she held out her wrists.

"Time to prove how big and tough you are."

Another good line, but she had no way of knowing he'd been worked over by experts far better at turning the guilt screws than she'd ever be.

"You're in my custody. For your own good."

"I'll bet that's what they said during the Inquisition," she said sweetly. Her tone hardened. "Do whatever you intend to do, Mr. Knight. Just don't hand me a line of bull about why you're doing it."

"My pleasure," he said grimly, and secured her wrists just as he had before.

Time crept by.

Cara sat staring out into the black sky. She was tired; she felt scruffy; she was hungry and, mostly, she was scared.

As for what had happened before, the body search... She wasn't going to think about it.

What her abductor had done. Her reaction. Her terror. Because that's what it had been, hadn't it? Terror? Fear, turned into acquiescence? A basic survival instinct at work?

It had to be. Because anything else was out of the—

"Ten minutes to touchdown."

She looked up, startled. Alexander Knight stood over her. How could a man his size move so quietly?

"Hungry?"

"No," she said coldly, "I'm not."

"Good." His smile didn't reach his eyes. "I forgot to order room service."

"You're a laugh a minute, Mr. Knight."

"Alex." Another of those icy smiles. "We really should drop the formalities, Ms. Prescott, wouldn't you agree?"

"I'm perfectly happy with form— What are you doing?" she said, jerking back as he bent toward her.

"I told you, we'll be landing soon. Time to untie you again."

She said nothing as he set her free, not even when he frowned and cupped one of her hands in his.

"You should have told me the belt was too tight."

"Why?" she said coldly. "Would that have added to your pleasure?"

Instead of answering, he rubbed his thumb lightly over the slight welt in her flesh. His touch was gentle. Soothing. She wanted to close her eyes, move closer, rest her head against his broad shoulder.

Instead, she yanked her hand away and turned her face to the window.

The plane had lost altitude, but though the blackness of night was giving way to the grayness that precedes dawn, there wasn't enough light yet to see anything on the ground. If only there were. She wanted, desperately, to see where they were going. A city? A town?

He sank into the seat beside hers. "The house is just a few minutes from the landing strip."

Don't ask. Don't give him the satisfaction.

But she did. "What house?" she heard herself say.

"My house." His jaw cracked as he yawned.

"You live in Florida?" God, what was the matter with her? Couldn't she keep her mouth shut?

"I live in Dallas. I bought this place a few months back. I haven't spent much time here yet."

An understatement, he thought, if ever there was one. He hadn't spent any time here at all, unless you counted a couple of weekends. He'd seen the island when he was down here on business, liked it and picked it up as an investment, maybe a weekend place, but he'd never thought beyond that.

"Is that the airport?"

Alex leaned toward the window. Lights illuminated the asphalt that stretched toward the horizon ahead of them.

"My airport, yeah."

She swung toward him. "*Your* airport?"

"It's a private island. *Isla de Palmas.*"

She stared at him. Then she turned away and pressed her forehead to the glass. What did she expect to see out there? A leper colony, from the way she clutched the arms of her seat.

The wheels kissed the runway. The plane ate up its length, then stopped. Alex got to his feet.

"Let's go."

Cara rose slowly. He could see the trepidation in her eyes. Good. Fine. The more wary she was of him and of this place, the better.

"Go where?"

"I told you. I own this place. Palm Island."

"You said there was a house."

"There is." He took her arm. She jerked away. His jaw tightened and he reached for her again, clamped his fingers around her elbow. "Don't give me a hard time, baby. You'll only regret it."

The door swung open. She blinked against the sudden glare of headlights, saw a man waiting at the foot of the steps. He was shorter and older than her abductor, but he had the same hard look about him.

"Alex," he said, as if she were invisible. "Good to see you, man."

"John. Sorry to get you up at such an ungodly hour."

"No problem. Everything is ready, just as you asked."

Everything is ready. Cara felt her heart kick into her throat. How could such simple words be so ominous?

Desperately, she wrenched free of Alex's grasp, scrambled down the steps and flung herself at the man called John. It was only later, when it no longer mattered, that she realized she hadn't gotten free at all, that Alex had simply let her go because he knew how useless her attempt would be.

"Help me! Please, please help me!" She grabbed his arm; she could hear Alex's steps behind her and knew she had only another few seconds before he reached her. "I've been kidnapped!"

Hard, masculine arms closed around her. She fought them but Alex's embrace was like steel.

"John owes me his life," he said coldly. "Nothing you can say will affect him."

"I'll kill you," Cara panted. "Damn you, I'll—"

Alex swung her into his arms, bent his head and took her mouth with his, kissing her over and over until, finally, he tasted the sweetness of her surrender.

"This is my island. Everything here belongs to me, Cara. Everything," he said thickly, "including you."

CHAPTER SIX

RAIN began to fall as the Jeep raced along a narrow asphalt road that followed the curve of the shoreline.

Alex held a trembling Cara in his arms.

A woman who'd played games with an organized crime boss, who'd told her government to get lost when it came to her for help, had every reason to tremble. He was doing what he had to do to keep her safe; if she was afraid of him, that was her problem.

Except—except, he could feel her heart racing against his, hear the accelerated shudder of her breath. Reluctantly, he let himself see the night through her eyes. How he'd broken into her apartment, dragged her from the shower, deliberately gone out of his way to establish control. It had been necessary: if he'd taken the time to try and explain things, they might both be dead by now.

One of the things you learned about survival was that there were times you had to do that which was expedient and worry about the consequences later. On that basis, he'd done a lot of things in his life he'd just as soon forget.

The Jeep bounced over a rut and his arms automatically tightened around Cara.

She was weeping. Very quietly, but he could hear it.

He slid his hand under her sweatshirt. She stiffened but he stroked her back, murmured soft nothings until he felt her shudder and droop against him.

He told himself that pleased him only because her compliance would make things easier, that it had nothing to do with the feel of her in his arms.

When they reached the house, John brought the Jeep to a stop. He started to get out, but Alex told him not to bother.

"We're fine," he said.

"Did I mention that the power's out?"

Alex laughed. "What else is new? I guess the generator I ordered didn't get here yet."

"Nope. I left candles in all the rooms and some sandwiches in the kitchen."

"Thanks. Now, go on. Get home before the weather really hits."

Alex stepped from the Jeep, Cara in his arms. The Jeep roared away, leaving them alone in the dark.

"I can walk."

He looked at her. The old defiance was back in her eyes but there was still a tremor in her voice. She was scared out of her skin and working hard not to show it.

"You're barefoot."

"This is Florida. People go around barefoot all the time."

He almost smiled at that little touch of bravado.

"Fine. Up the steps. Good. Now just stand there while I unlock the door. And, by the way, don't even think about it."

Her head jerked toward him. "Think about what?" she said carefully.

"Even if you found John's cabin, he'd just bring you back to me." Alex took his keys from his pocket, selected one and inserted it into the door lock. "Besides, you'd probably stumble into the swamp before you found his place. We have some impressive alligators on the island. Did I mention that before?"

He was lying. He was, wasn't he? He had to be. Still, Cara cast an inadvertent look at her bare feet.

"In you go," he said, as the door swung open.

The house wasn't just dark, it was black. She took a step forward, thought about alligators and stopped. Alex propelled her forward another step.

"We get snakes in the house sometimes, not gators."

Another lie. It had to be, but just in case it wasn't, could a person curl her toes up into her armpits?

Something scratched. Hissed. A candle flamed to life. Cara's gaze swept over the floor. A sea of pale hardwood. A brilliantly colored rug.

No snakes.

"No snakes," she said. "And, I'd bet, no alligators." She eyed him narrowly. "What's next? Stories about the bogeyman?"

He moved past her, using the candle to bring a candelabra to life.

"I don't deal in fantasy," he said coolly. "Some of the things that make up my reality are fantastic enough. Are you hungry?"

She was starved. "No."

"Thirsty?"

She was parched. "No."

"That's too bad. I guess you're just going to have to suffer through watching me eat those sandwiches John mentioned."

Her stomach growled. It would snarl if she had to watch him eat.

"You said we were going straight to bed."

He looked at her, a slow smile curving his mouth. Heat shot into her face.

"I only meant—I meant—" Cara swallowed dryly. "I'd like to wash up."

"Good idea. Showers first. Dry, clean clothes. Then we'll have supper."

"I don't want supper."

"Yeah. So you said." He put his hand in the small of her back again. "Let's go."

"Go where?"

"Upstairs."

"What for?"

Alex's eyes narrowed. So much for those quick moments of feeling sorry for her.

"Okay," he said, clasping her shoulders and swinging her to him, "let's get this straight. I'm tired as hell and my belly's empty. I feel like I've been living in this shirt and jeans for the last hundred years, and a little guy with a pair of drumsticks just started tapping out a beat in my skull." His hands tightened on her. "The last thing I need is to deal with a whiny ten-year-old. I tell you something, just shut up and do it."

"I only asked—"

"Oh, for God's sake!" Glowering, he scooped her into his arms and went up the stairs, ignoring her yelp of protest. The door facing them was half closed; he shouldered it open, strode inside and dumped her on her feet. A few seconds later, a yellow candle flame glowed against the darkness.

"Do something useful," he growled. "Take some matches and light those other candles."

"Are you sure you trust me?" Cara said sweetly. "If I'm only ten…"

"Light the damned candles!"

She did, not for his benefit but for hers. She wanted a look at her prison. Well, she thought, on a hitch of breath, all right. Calling it a "prison" was a bit of an overstatement. They were in an enormous bedroom, complete with a fireplace and a big, four-poster bed.

"Satisfied with the accommodations?"

Cara swung around. Alex had come up behind her, as soundlessly as a big cat.

"Don't do that," she said irritably.

"Ask if you're satisfied?"

"Don't sneak around. I don't like it."

"Anything else you want to complain about while you're at it?"

There was a dangerous glint in his eye but she was too tired to give a damn.

"Yes. I want to know why you brought me here."

"I told you. It's a safe place."

"New York was a safe place."

"Well, sure, if you discount the camera, the listening devices and, oh, let's not forget the goon who broke into your apartment and the other one who was waiting in the street."

Maybe he was right, but the bottom line was that she had no reason to trust him. For all she knew, the camera was a setup. So were the bugs in the phones. And the so-called "goons" might have been sent to protect her.

She told him all that.

Alex's eyes narrowed. "You think I was lying about the camera and the bugs?"

"I think it was awfully convenient, you finding those devices just when you needed me to think you were Sir Galahad."

He laughed. "Sweetheart, you have a very creative mind. And what about that pair of creeps? Or do you think they were Boy Scouts sent to protect you?"

She knew he was right. She didn't really believe he'd set things up and she certainly didn't believe the men he'd knocked out were there to protect her.

Nobody was interested in protecting her. They all wanted something from her, something she didn't have to give. All of them, including this man.

"Those guys wanted to hurt you, baby. Hell, why dance around the truth? The odds are they wanted to kill you."

"And you don't?" Her voice was soft and small.

A muscle knotted in his jaw. He thought about reaching out, pulling her against him. Telling her she didn't have to be afraid, that he'd protect her….

Protect her from the mob boss she'd slept with? The federal prosecutor she'd refused to help?

Five minutes out from under his thumb and she'd managed to get him feeling sorry for her. It was an easy step from there to making him do something stupid.

That wasn't going to happen.

He reached back, his eyes never leaving hers, and shut the door.

"Wait a minute," she said. "Alex…"

"I'm Alex now, am I, baby? Good. Excellent, in fact, considering that it's time to get undressed."

The fear in her eyes now was bright and real.

"What?"

"What's the problem? You having difficulty under-standing English?" His voice hardened. "I said, get your clothes off."

"All that nonsense about protecting me..." Her voice trembled and broke. "Protecting me from what? From whom? Here we are, alone in the middle of nowhere, and I see how much your protection is worth."

"You've got a dirty mind, babe." Alex toed off his boots. "We need to clean up. I'm only interested in saving water."

She wanted to laugh. How many horny guys had used that line to try to get a woman to share a shower? Somehow, she'd expected more from him.

"The power's off, remember? I don't know when it'll come on again. The water tank's big but every minute we stand around, the temp of that water drops a little more."

"I am not taking my clothes off!"

She lurched forward. Alex put a hand out, wrapped it lightly around her jaw and held her in place.

"Yeah," he said coldly, "you are. I'm tired, my jeans and shirt damn near need to be burned. I want a hot shower, clean clothes, some food in my belly and a warm bed, not another earful of nonsense."

Desperate, she searched for a way to buy time. "We've lost our audience," she said. "First the cop, then the pilot, now your pal, John. Is there any point in playing to an empty house?"

"Is that what you think I'm doing?"

His eyes held hers. Somehow, she kept from scram-bling away as he lay his hand between her breasts. She didn't react, even though she could sense the coiled power of his long, hard body in that light touch.

"Your heart's racing."

"Don't worry about it."

"Ah, but you're my responsibility. Got to keep you safe, remember?"

Tension hung in the air, thick as the cloud of thunder that rumbled over the ocean, louder than the sound of her galloping heart.

"You want me to believe you work for the government. Well, I don't."

"So, what are you telling me, sweetheart?" He grinned. "That you'd get undressed for a fed but not for me?"

Was she supposed to laugh? Not when her life was at stake. No matter what he said, he wasn't a federal agent. She hadn't dealt with many of Uncle Sam's functionaries but she knew what the two who'd visited her had looked like. They'd been cold-faced men wearing phony smiles and dark suits, not hunks of solid masculinity in T-shirts and jeans.

They didn't touch a woman and make her feel— make her feel—

Cara shook free of Alex's hand and took a few steps back. "I wouldn't care if you were Elvis. I might be your prisoner but I'm not a slave."

His eyebrows lifted. He looked around the room slowly, as if it were as new to him as it was to her.

"Must be one hell of a disappointment, expecting steel bars and ending up in something like this."

His sarcasm made her wince, but giving an inch would be the same as giving a mile.

"Iron bars do not a prison make," she said coldly.

"It's stone walls. 'Stone walls do not a prison make, nor iron bars a cage.'" His smile thinned. "Gotta get it right, if you really want to impress the peasants."

She knew her mouth had dropped open. She couldn't help it. Alexander Knight, quoting an obscure seventeenth-century poet?

"Unpleasant, isn't it?"

His voice had gone low, his smile dangerous and very male. Cara told herself to hold her ground.

"What's unpleasant?"

"Being labeled."

"I don't know what you mean."

He reached out slowly, took a fistful of her sweatshirt and tugged her forward. She stumbled and ended up an inch from his big, hard body.

This close, she could see that his green eyes flashed with specks of gold. That his jaw was dark with stubble. What would it feel like, under her fingertips? Rough, she thought, rough and delicious and sexy, incredibly sexy against her hands, her throat...

"You've written me off as something a lady like you wouldn't want anywhere near her."

"That isn't—"

She caught her breath as his hands closed on her shoulders.

"Yeah. It is. And that's really amazing, because you're not a lady. You're Tony's property. A Mafia princess, looking down on the man sent to keep her safe."

"You don't know anything about me." Her voice quavered; she hated herself for it but she didn't like being so close to him, having his breath warm on her face, his hands hard on her shoulders. "And I don't believe you've been sent to keep me safe."

"Didn't we have this discussion already? I keep telling you that I'm not here to hurt you."

"But you've done things like that," Cara said, her eyes steady on his. "You've hurt people."

Something changed in him. She could see it, feel it, an almost palpable presence in the room. Silence stretched between them, a yawning chasm she could not cross, and she knew, looking at his face, that she had made a terrible mistake.

"Alex," she said. "Alex, I didn't mean—"

"Is that what you want?" he said in a low voice. "Rough sex with a man like me?"

"No!" She stumbled back. "I didn't mean—"

"Yeah. You did. That's the message you've been sending out. I was just too dumb to get it."

"You're wrong. I didn't—"

"Get your clothes off." His hands went to his belt, the same belt he'd used to tie her wrists. "It's time, Cara. You know it as well as I do."

God, oh, God, this couldn't be happening! "Please! I don't want—"

"The hell you don't."

The belt slid open; his hands went to the button at the top of his fly. Her gaze dropped, the breath catching in her throat when she saw the hard bulge beneath the taut denim.

"This has been coming from the minute we saw each other." His mouth twisted. "And I'm tired of waiting."

He reached for her. She kicked. Punched. Fought him, hard, but he was too big, too powerful, too filled with cold rage.

She couldn't stop him.

He crushed her mouth beneath his, slid his hands under her sweatshirt, lowered his head and sucked one tightly budded nipple into his mouth.

Just that—his mouth on her breast—and sensation

shot through her, hot and shocking as wildfire. She cried out; her knees buckled and Alex swept her into his arms and carried her to the bed.

He came down on it with her still in his arms, his mouth at her breast again, torturing her with his lips, his tongue, his teeth. Cara arched toward him, reason gone, nothing but red-hot desire pounding through her veins.

"Yes," he growled, "yes. Like that. Just like that."

He pulled down her sweatpants, lifted her to him, moved against her, driving the power of his aroused flesh against the place between her thighs that wept for his possession.

For his possession.

The realization almost stopped her breath.

Her eyes flew open. She saw the exciting, beautiful, mindlessly intent face above hers. The face of a stranger who had all but just told her he was a killer.

"No." The word came out a whisper. "No!" she screamed, frantic now, aware of his strength, his size. She shoved at his chest. At his shoulders. "Get away from me!"

For a moment that seemed to stretch into infinity, he didn't move. His powerful body pinned hers to the bed and she thought, *He can do whatever he wants to me now.*

He could.

There was no one to stop him.

What if he did? What if he tied her hands to the bedposts? Took what he wanted? What if she had no choice but to surrender to him? To his passion and, yes, to hers?

Her heart pounded. She could feel her bones melting. Maybe it showed in her eyes because, suddenly, he rolled away.

"I've done a lot of things I'm not proud of in my life, Ms. Prescott," he said in a tone she knew she'd always remember, "but rape isn't one of them, not even when it's meant to accommodate a woman who'd rather be forced than admit she wants to get laid."

Cara shot up from the bed and cracked her hand across his cheek. His head flew back; he caught her wrist, twisted it behind her hard enough to make her cry out.

"That's twice," he said softly. "You're playing with fire, Cara. Don't. Not unless you're looking to get burned."

She knew better than to answer. After a few seconds, he stood up, his jeans riding low on his hips.

"You'll find whatever you need in the bathroom." His eyes were hard as glass. "Towels, shampoo, toothbrush, a robe. Mine," he said, with a swift, wolfish show of teeth. "But then, I wasn't planning on a female guest."

The door slammed shut behind him. Cara shuddered and fell back on the bed.

Hours dragged by.

Thunder rolled overhead. Lightning slashed the sky. The storm was upon the island, rain and wind beating against the house with primitive fury.

When she was little, she'd hated thunderstorms. She had only vague memories of those years, and of her father. How he'd come into her room, sit by her bed and reassure her.

Cara, he'd say in his gruff voice, *mia figlia, you must learn to be brave. Nothing can hurt you unless you permit it.*

She'd never really believed him.

Her parents had divorced. That had hurt. Her mother

had died. That hurt, too. And then, one morning, she looked up from her desk in the library, saw a man looking at her, a man who smiled and said, *My name is Anthony Gennaro.*

And, that quickly, her life had changed. Turned into a complex series of twists and turns. Black was white; white was black. The good guys turned into the bad guys with dazzling speed.

Who was Alex? Was he good…or was he bad?

How could she want to make love with a man like him? Because he was right. She could, at least, be honest with herself, couldn't she?

She wanted to go to bed with him. Wanted to feel his body bearing down on hers. Wanted to feel him deep inside her. Wanted to cry out as he took her.

And the terrible truth was, she didn't care what he was. If he was good, if he was bad. He was so beautiful. So savagely male.

Wanting him was enough.

She'd never felt this way before. Boneless, when he looked at her, his green eyes dark and hot. Breathless, when he kissed her. And, yes, safe when he held her, safe in his arms, even though that was crazy.

Plus, she didn't sleep around. There'd been one man. Only one until tonight, and she wasn't going to change that, wasn't going to give in to some—some sick fantasy.

Wasn't, wasn't, wasn't…

The bedroom door flew open. As it did, a jagged streak of lightning illuminated Alex, standing in the doorway, shoulders filling it.

"Cara."

His voice was rough. The sound of it, the sight of

him, a beautiful predator now fueled not by rage but by desire, and she knew she was lost.

"Alex," she whispered.

Their eyes met, and she flew to him.

His arms wrapped around her. He clasped her face in his hands and kissed her, angling his mouth over hers again and again as he pushed her back against the wall.

"Tell me what you want," he growled.

"You," she said, "you, you—"

He groaned, kissed her again and she opened her mouth to his pillaging tongue. He nipped the soft flesh of her bottom lip, nipped her throat and she moaned and rubbed herself against him, wanting this, wanting him, more than she wanted life.

She reached between them, cupped her hand over his erection, felt it straining against the rough denim of his jeans.

He said something low and urgent, told her what he was going to do to her in blunt, Anglo-Saxon terms that made her lift her mouth for another soul-shattering kiss.

Then he unzipped his jeans, dragged down her sweat-pants, lifted her in his arms and thrust into her.

Her cry of pleasure, the almost instantaneous contractions of her muscles as they spasmed around him, almost destroyed his control. Sweat beaded his knotted muscles as he held her against the wall, as he drove into her again, put his hand between them, found her slick heat and caressed her until she sobbed his name and came again in his arms.

Then, only then, Alex let go. Came on one long, impossibly long rush of ecstasy, his head back, his lips drawn away from his teeth. Spilled himself into her until logic said there could be nothing left.

To hell with logic.

"Cara," he whispered, and he lifted her in his arms and carried her to the bed, still inside her, still hard...

Still wanting her.

CHAPTER SEVEN

THE bedroom was silent, except for Cara's soft moans as Alex made love to her.

He withdrew from her slowly. God, so slowly it made him tremble. She reached for him but he took her hands, kissed the palms, kissed her mouth and told her they had all the time in the world now.

Time to explore.

To taste her honeyed mouth. Her skin. Her throat, there, just at the hollow and there, at the juncture of neck and shoulder. That made her purr with contentment and he did it again, nipping her lightly, then soothing the small hurt with his tongue.

And, all the while, he cupped her breasts with his hands.

Ran his thumbs over her nipples. Groaned at her swift response to the gentle torment and, finally, lowered his mouth to taste their sweetness.

To taste her nipples, pale rose and beaded, eager for the heat of his mouth.

God, she had beautiful breasts.

He loved the silken feel of them. The way they fit his hands. The way she arched her back when he sucked her nipples into his mouth.

And those sounds she made.

They were enough to take him over the edge but he wouldn't let that happen. Not this time. He wanted to make this last. To kiss all of her. Taste all of her. Then, only then, would he kneel between her thighs and possess her again.

Slowly, he moved down Cara's body, kissing, sucking, licking her flesh while she twisted with excitement beneath him, taking the clean, woman-scent of her deep into his nostrils, stroking her belly, circling her navel with the tip of his tongue.

"Alex," she whispered. She reached for him again, her hands clutching at his shoulders, and there was something in the whispered word, in her questioning touch, something so sweet and, yes, so innocent that it sent a shudder of pleasure through him.

"Yes, baby," he said softly, and slid his fingers through the soft, gold-tipped curls that guarded her feminine heart.

And touched her.

A wild cry that started in the very center of her burst from her throat. He looked up at her face, watched the shock, the pleasure turn her eyes wide, and something fierce roared in his blood.

"Do you like this?" he said thickly.

"Oh God," she whispered. "Alex. Alex—"

He parted her with his fingertips. Saw how beautiful she was. The petals of her labia. The pink bud of her clitoris.

He cupped her bottom, lifted her to him and stroked her with his tongue. Her cry rang out in the silence of the room; her hands dug into his hair.

Her taste was exquisite; it rocketed through him and

when she cried out and came against his mouth, he thought his heart might explode with pleasure.

He lifted his head, wanting to see her face at this moment, wanting to see her eyes, yes, dark like that. Her hair, yes, wild against his pillows. Her skin flushed and damp and, God, he wanted more, more…

She reached for him.

"Alex." Her voice shook. "Come into me. I want you inside me."

The soft plea, the touch of her hand, pushed him to the edge. He rolled away from her, dug in the nightstand drawer while he sent up a fevered prayer he'd stashed condoms in it even though he'd never had a woman here until now.

Yes. He found the small packets. Tore one open. Rolled it on and decided not to think about the fact that he hadn't used one the first time.

He kissed her, deeply. Whispered that she was beautiful. And sank into her as slowly as the fever gripping him would allow. He wanted this moment to last forever. The heat of her around him. The softness of her beneath him. Her little cries as he filled her.

When he was deep, deep inside her, he began to move.

Slowly still. Each stroke almost more than he could take.

He could feel the thud of his heart and hers. The contractions of her body as she rose to his thrusts. The world was fracturing around him. He couldn't think. There was only this. This. This…

Cara cried out and clung to him.

"I can't," she said. "I can't…"

"Don't be afraid," he whispered. "I'm here. I'm with you. I won't let you fall."

He felt it happen. The pulsing of her womb. And as she cried out, he let go, let go of everything and flew with her into the starlit universe.

Cara awoke.

The bed. The room. The open balcony door and the sea breeze blowing gently on her skin.

Her naked skin.

Her mind was a jumble of confused thoughts, starting with what had happened in her apartment and ended here, in this room…

In this bed.

She shot up against the pillows. Was he here? The stranger who'd made love to her? She looked around wildly, heart galloping until she was sure she was alone.

Unless he was in the attached bathroom.

No. The door was open; the room was empty.

Her relief didn't last long. He wasn't here but she still had to face him, and how was she going to manage that? This was the twenty-first century and women slept with men they'd just met all the time.

But she didn't. She never had. Tending a sick mother, working after school from the time she was fourteen, then working her way through college hadn't left much time for dating or boys.

She'd had sex twice in her entire life, each time with the same man. He was the director of the university library where she'd worked after she got her degree. He was a nice guy, pleasant and soft-spoken.

The first time had been awkward. She'd undressed on one side of the bed, he on the other; they'd climbed under the blankets with the lights out. A couple of kisses. A couple of caresses. Then the main event.

It had been an awful disappointment.

Looking back, she wondered if they'd only tried again because they needed to prove that sex could be better than that.

If so, they'd failed. Miserably.

The second attempt had been pitiful. Worse than the first. It was hard to know who'd been more embarrassed, she or he.

Well, there'd been nothing pitiful about what had happened in this bed last night. But embarrassing?

Heat rose in Cara's face.

Humiliating, was more like it. They'd had sex against the wall. *Against the wall!* She hadn't even known you could do that. Hadn't known you could do other things, too. That a man could put his mouth against your…

Not any man. Alex. Her tall, dark, gorgeously dangerous captor.

Cara shut her eyes.

Maybe that was the worst of it. That she didn't even know him. Where he came from. Where he lived. What he did besides break into people's houses and abduct them.

The only thing she knew was that he was an incredible lover. Demanding, yet giving. Powerful, yet gentle. He'd taught her things about her own body…

Just remembering made heat pool low in her belly. She'd never dreamed sex could be like this. That you could shatter like crystal in your lover's arms.

Except, Alex wasn't her lover.

He was a dangerous stranger. Who held her prisoner on an island that might as well have been a million miles from nowhere.

Now, she had to face him.

Good morning, hello, nice weather we're hav-

ing…and oh, by the way, what happened last night was one huge mistake and it won't happen again.

Cara sat up and pushed aside the covers. The sooner she got this over with, the better.

The power was back on.

She took a long, hot shower. Alex must have taken one, too. The stall was still steamy; the soap was damp. She picked it up, held it to her nose and imagined that it smelled like him, that she could still smell him on her….

But not for long.

She scrubbed from head to toe, washing away the scent of sex. Of Alex.

He'd left a new toothbrush on the sink for her. That didn't surprise her.

A man who made love with such expertise would keep toothbrushes on hand for all the women who passed through his life. The same for the condoms in the night table drawer.

She tried not to think about that first time, when he hadn't used a condom. Unprotected sex? What had she been thinking?

The answer, of course, was that she hadn't been thinking at all.

Her clothes were gone. In their place she found a pair of denim cutoffs and a T-shirt. Both were Alex's. She could tell by the way they fit. Actually, the way they didn't fit. The shorts could have held two of her, even fastened with a safety pin she found in one of the vanity drawers, and the shirt hung below her knees.

She thought about skipping the shorts until she remembered she had no panties.

Then she thought about how that would be. Wearing only the T-shirt and knowing she was naked beneath it.

Alex wouldn't know, not unless she wanted him to.

Not unless she brushed up against him a couple of times, or—or bent to pick up something from the floor....

In a heartbeat, she felt herself turn soft and liquid and ready for sex. For Alex. For the feel of him, deep inside her.

Cara frowned, took a deep breath and headed downstairs.

The house was beautiful.

It was big and, she sensed, old enough to have a rich history. Ceiling fans turned lazily against the high ceilings; silk oriental rugs glittered like jewels against the pale hardwood floors. The furniture was Scandinavian, almost shockingly contemporary against the antique rugs and yet, somehow, perfectly suited to them.

Still, the rooms lacked something. A personal touch. There were none of the little things people stash on tables and hang on walls to say, *This place is mine.* It was as if nobody actually lived here.

"Nobody does."

Cara spun around. Alex stood in the living room archway, arms folded, feet crossed at the ankles. He was wearing denim cutoffs, leather sandals, a faded Dallas Cowboys shirt with the sleeves cut out...

And an expression that was absolutely unreadable.

It wasn't easy, but somehow, she managed a polite smile.

"Did I—did I say that out loud?"

"Uh-huh. And you're right. Nobody lives here."

She nodded. This was good. They were having a conversation instead of being trapped halfway between *Good morning* and *Just look at all that sunshine*!

"Ah," she said brightly. "I guess I misunderstood you last night."

A little smile kicked up one corner of his mouth. "Oh, I thought you understood me pretty well."

The tone of his voice was pure sex. Cara felt her face heat. Talk about making foolish remarks...

"I meant," she said carefully, "I thought you'd said this was your house."

"It is. I bought it a few months back and furnished it." Another lazy smile. "Well, I had a decorator furnish it. The same guy who did my condo in Dallas. But I've never actually lived here. I've flown out for a couple of weekends, is all."

"Oh," she said, while she tried frantically to process everything. This man, who'd traded his jeans and sneakers for a pair of denim shorts and beat-up leather sandals, not only owned this house, he also owned a Dallas condo?

"Cara?"

"Yes?"

"What else do you want to know?"

Her eyes shot to his face. The smile was gone, replaced by an intensity that seemed capable of burning straight through to the marrow of her bones.

"I don't know what you mean."

"Sure you do," he said softly. "You slept with me last night and you woke up this morning thinking it had been one hell of a mistake."

He was saying exactly what she'd been going to say.

That was good, wasn't it? Except—except, it hadn't been a mistake. Sleeping with him had been—it had been incredible.

Hadn't it been that way for him, too?

"Worse, you realized you don't know a damned thing about me. Right?"

Cara nodded. It was the safest thing to do.

"Well," he said gruffly, "you're right. You don't know me. I don't know you, or maybe I should say, what we do know about each other isn't very flattering." He paused; she could see a muscle dance in his jaw. "You probably think I'm a stone-cold son of a bitch who rides roughshod over people. Over women. And all I know about you is that your taste in men isn't anything to write home about."

God, he was insufferable! That self-righteous tone… How could she have been foolish enough to have fallen into bed with him?

"You're right," she said coolly, "about me and my taste in men—otherwise, I'd never have ended up giving in to you last night."

He was across the room so fast she barely had time to take a quick step back.

"You're not listening, damn it!" He caught hold of her shoulders, shook her as he drew her to her toes. "I'm trying to tell you that it's true. We don't know anything about each other."

"And I said you were right."

"You didn't let me finish." He drew a rough breath. "Maybe, just maybe, what we think we know isn't accurate."

Did he think he could make things better with word games?

"You're wrong. What I know about you is far too accurate. You're just what you said you were, a stone-cold son of a—"

His mouth swooped down on hers. She gasped, slapped her hands against his chest, but he gathered her against him, trapped her hands between his body and hers. She tried to twist her face away but he cupped the back of her head, his fingers hard against her scalp, and refused to let her escape his kiss.

"Bastard," she said against his mouth. "No-good bast—"

"Shut up and kiss me," he whispered.

No, she told herself, *no, no, no…*

Cara wound her arms around her lover's neck and kissed him back with all the passion so long held prisoner in her heart.

Alex scooped her into his arms…

And carried her to the kitchen, where he settled her on a stool at a white counter and paused for one quick, deep kiss.

"Guess what happens now?" he said softly, against her mouth.

Her lips curved in a smile that elicited a low, wicked chuckle.

"Not yet. First we eat. Breakfast or lunch or supper or whatever meal you want to call it. Neither of us has eaten in—help me out here, babe. Is it one week or two?"

Cara laughed. That delighted him. He had never heard her laugh before. How could he feel as if he'd known her all his life and not have heard her laugh until now?

"You can cook?"

"You're going to regret such skepticism, Ms.

Prescott. Of course, I can cook. I'm a bachelor. How do you think I survive?"

"With a freezer full of TV dinners."

"Well, sure. And takeout." Alex opened the fridge and looked inside. "And leftovers, thanks to sisters-in-law who figure I'd starve to death without their help."

"You have brothers?"

"Uh-huh." He turned around, a dozen eggs in one hand, a pound of bacon in the other. "Two. Don't look so surprised, sweetheart. I'm as human as anybody else."

Cara blushed. "I didn't mean—"

"Yeah. You did, and nobody could blame you." He opened a cabinet, took out two skillets and put them on top of a stove better suited to a restaurant. "Okay," he said, laying out strips of bacon in one skillet and turning on the flame beneath it. "Here're the pertinent details. Alexander Knight. Well, you already know that. Age thirty. I live in Dallas where I'm in partnership with my brothers in something we call Risk Management Specialists but until a few years ago, I worked for the federal agency that asked me to keep an eye on you."

"And in your world," Cara said carefully, "that means what, exactly?"

Alex broke all the eggs into a huge bowl, added milk and began whipping them to a froth.

"It means doing whatever it takes to keep someone safe."

"And, right now, I'm that someone?"

"Yes."

"And—and if the subject is female, do you always sle—"

He kissed her before she could finish the sentence.

"No," he said gruffly, "I damned well do not! I've gone against all the rules, making love with you…but I don't care." He reached out, traced her lips with the tip of his finger. "The truth is," he said softly, "I knew I wanted you from the minute I saw you."

Cara caught his hand and brought it to her mouth. "I thought you'd been sent to kill me," she said, so quietly he had to strain to hear her.

"That son of a bitch Gennaro." Alex's mouth twisted. "I ever get my hands on him—"

"Not by him. He wouldn't—"

She'd said the wrong thing. One look at his narrowed eyes and she knew it.

"Alex. I didn't mean—"

"Forget it."

"No. Please. You don't understand."

He swung toward her, his expression frightening. "I understand, all right."

"You don't!"

"Tony G still owns you."

"That's not true!"

"The hell it isn't!"

He started toward the kitchen door, his steps long and purposeful. Cara stared at his rigid back. Then she launched herself off the stool and went after him.

"I was right," she said, slamming her fist into his shoulder. "You really are a self-righteous son of a bitch!"

Alex turned and faced her. "Be careful," he said softly. "Remember what I told you about playing with fire?"

"Anthony Gennaro was not my lover!"

"No?" His voice was cold. "What was he, then? Your own private version of Santa Claus?"

She stared at him, hating him for what he believed, hating herself for letting it matter...

And wishing she could tell him the truth.

"No answer, baby?" He flashed a quick smile. "No problem. It's a big house. There are three guest suites. Pick one. With luck, we'll stay out of each other's way until this is over."

"Until what's over?" Cara said furiously. "The FBI wants me to testify about something and I don't know what it is. Somebody wants to kill me and I don't know who it is. You—you charge into my life, turn it upside down, tell me Anthony Gennaro owns me and then— and then you seduce me anyway—"

Her voice broke. She stared at him, eyes blind with despair, then spun away.

"Cara."

"Leave me alone, Alex. I don't want to talk to you anymore."

He didn't want to talk to her, either. Of all the god-damned times to tell him she was still hung up on Anthony Gennaro...

Except, she hadn't said that. All she'd done was defend Gennaro against his assertion that the *capo* wanted her dead. If she couldn't bring herself to believe that, how could he blame her? Hell, she'd been Gennaro's lover...

She said she hadn't been that, either.

Maybe it was true. Or maybe it wasn't. Maybe it just didn't matter. Last night, she'd felt so right in his arms. So innocent in the ways she'd responded to him.

Her past hadn't mattered, then. Why should it matter now?

Alex cleared his throat. "Cara?"

"Go away."

Her voice trembled. All of her was trembling. It killed him to see her like this, hurt and alone and afraid.

He took a step toward her. "Cara."

Still no answer. When he reached her, he put his hands lightly on her shoulders.

"Baby. I'm sorry. I shouldn't have said those things."

"You think them. That's what matters."

Slowly, he turned her toward him. She resisted. Then, gradually, he felt her yielding.

"Sweetheart. Look at me."

She raised her head. His heart turned over when he saw the tears in her eyes.

"I was jealous," he said simply. "You defended Gennaro and I thought—hell, I thought, even after last night, even after all those hours in my arms, she's still thinking about another man."

"I'm not like that," she said, chin lifted, mouth set, every line of her body a testament to her strength and determination.

"No," he said slowly, "you aren't. I should have realized that, but I didn't." Alex hesitated. "We're going to be here for a while. Could we—do you think we could get to know each other a little?"

"You don't have to know me to keep me safe," she said.

The words were simple but he knew that what lay beneath them was far more complicated.

"Yeah," he said softly, "I do."

"Why?"

He put his arms around her. "Because something's happening here, sweetheart. I don't know what it is, but I'll be damned if I'm going to turn away from it, or let you turn away from it, until we get it all figured out."

It wasn't a commitment. Not by a long shot, but it was closer to one than he'd ever made to a woman in his life.

It was crazy.

He didn't know Cara. She didn't know him. He'd told her that only a little while ago, and it was the God's honest truth.

And yet—and yet, this felt right. Cara, in his arms. Her sweet mouth, as he took it in a long, deep kiss. Her sigh, as it mingled with his breath.

Alex lifted her into his arms. He carried her past the stove, picked up the skillet full of charred bacon and dumped it into the sink.

If the house was going to go up in flames, it wouldn't be because of a pan of bacon.

It would be because of what happened when she was in his bed.

CHAPTER EIGHT

THEY made love in ways Cara had read about but never imagined could be real.

Alex lifted her on top of him. Brought her down slowly on his erection, slowly enough that she could watch his eyes darken as she took him inside her, feel her muscles stretch to accommodate him.

He was big. Wonderfully big and, at first, seeing him in the revealing light of late morning, she'd wondered if their coupling were possible.

Her thoughts must have been easy to read because he'd grinned wickedly as he rolled her beneath him and reminded her that they'd fit together perfectly the night before.

And, oh, they fit together perfectly now.

When she was beneath him. When she rode him. When he put his arm around her waist, drew her back against him and entered her from behind.

Maybe it was old-fashioned, but lying under him was what she loved best. She'd gone toe to toe with men in the real world, had stood up to FBI agents and Anthony Gennaro…

But she loved the feeling of being possessed by Alex. Of being taken by him.

She loved everything he taught her about making love.

About love.

About loving him.

And when that thought tiptoed into her mind as she lay, spent and happy, in the curve of his arms, Cara pushed it away. Nobody had mentioned love. Nobody would. She was naïve about sex and men, but she wasn't stupid.

This had nothing to do with love. It was too quick, too unreal. Besides, a man like Alex wouldn't fall in love with a woman like her.

Under any other circumstances, without all the attendant elements of danger, he wouldn't have looked at her twice.

She knew that.

Besides, she hardly knew him. You couldn't fall in love with a stranger.

Could you?

The sun was sinking toward the horizon when Alex groaned like a man in pain.

Cara raised her head from his shoulder and stared at him. "What's the matter?"

"I'm dying," he replied, so dramatically she knew it wasn't true.

The corners of her mouth lifted in a smile. "From what?"

"Starvation," he gasped. He took her hand and put it on his ridged belly. "See? I'm nothing but skin and bones."

"Mmm," she said, and moved her hand lower. "Wait a minute. What's this?"

She squealed as he rolled her beneath him. "If you don't know what that is, Red Riding Hood, I'm just going to have to show you." She laughed softly as he smiled at her. "Seriously, sweetheart. I'm starving."

"So am I. What're we going to do about it?"

"Well…we could send out for pizza, but—"

"But?"

"Delivery would take a couple of hours."

Smiling, Cara linked her hands behind his neck. "Didn't we have breakfast?" she said dreamily. "I thought you made bacon and eggs."

Alex took a mock-ferocious nip of her shoulder. "The bacon burned, thanks to you."

"To me?" she said, batting her lashes.

"I'm warning you, woman. Get your mind on food or John's going to find our skeletons in the morning."

"Okay. No pizza. What other choices do I have?"

"A sail to the mainland for dinner."

"And that would take how long?"

"Showering, getting dressed, hoping for a good following wind with the spinnaker up. In other words, the same couple of hours."

"So, we're destined to starve?"

"Well…" Smiling, he brushed his lips over hers. "If I remember correctly, there are steaks in the freezer. And I'll bet John put fixings for a salad in the refrigerator." Cara's stomach growled. Alex laughed, gave her another quick kiss and swung his legs to the floor. He grabbed his cutoffs, took her hand and tugged her to her feet. "I'm assuming that was a 'yes' vote for dinner at home."

She smiled. "You do the steaks. I'll do the salad. Hey!" She dug her feet in as Alex drew her to the door. "I can't go downstairs like this."

He looked at her. She was naked, her skin rosy from

hours of lovemaking, her hair tangled and wild and incredibly sexy.

"Like how?" he said, with an innocence ruined by the gleam in his eye.

"Like—like this," Cara answered, and when she blushed, he knew he wanted to say to hell with dinner, even though he was starving, to hell with everything except tumbling her onto the bed.

Smiling, he drew her into his arms.

"You look beautiful," he said softly.

"So do you."

He grinned, she blushed again, and he felt something tilt in the vicinity of his heart.

"But I can't go downstairs without clothes."

"Why?"

He asked the question so reasonably that, for a moment, Cara had to search for an answer.

"Well—well, someone might see."

"Me. I'll see. And I like the view of you naked just fine."

"John—"

"Never comes to the house when I'm here without calling first. And don't get that look on your face, baby. It has to do with me liking my privacy, not with my choice in guests." Alex hesitated. He had no idea why he wanted to tell her this, but he did. "Anyway, I've never brought a woman here until now."

"The condoms…"

Could a woman really blush this many times? "Habit," he said simply. "Keep 'em beside the bed, you never forget to put one on… Except for last night." He hesitated. "I've never forgotten before," he said, voice gruff and yet, somehow, tender. Instinct told him not remembering the condom had less to do with forgetting and more to do with something else. He'd tried to reason it through but couldn't. Besides, right now, what he owed her was reassurance. "I'm healthy, Cara. You have the right to know that."

"So am I. And—and this is my safe time of month." She gave a little laugh and buried her face in his shoulder. "Don't look at me like that!"

"I can't help it. I thought women gave up blushing about the time they gave up corsets."

"I wish I didn't blush. It's awful."

"It's wonderful." He framed her face with his hands, lifted it to his and kissed her, loving the way she leaned into him as if he were all that she needed in the world. The kiss lasted a long time; he only ended it because he knew if he didn't, they'd never leave the bedroom, and they needed food. Energy. Not only so he could make love to her forever, but in case...

In case something happened.

Hell. He had to check the house, check in with John. He'd damned near let the danger she was in slip his mind. And she *was* in danger; that pair of goons in New York hadn't been there to pay a social visit.

That was the problem with mixing business and pleasure. You lost focus. Your attention wandered. And if anything happened to this woman—if he let anything happen to her...

Alex stepped back. "Okay," he said gruffly. "Put on my robe and we'll go down and make dinner."

They dressed, Cara in a terry-cloth robe that came down to her toes, Alex in jeans and a T-shirt. Yes, there were steaks in the freezer; red leaf lettuce and tiny grape tomatoes in the bottom drawer of the refrigerator.

They worked in what should have been companionable silence—Alex defrosting the steaks in the microwave oven, Cara washing the lettuce, shredding it into a wooden bowl and putting together a dressing—but a sudden tension had crept in.

Something was wrong, Cara knew, but what?

Night had fallen by the time everything was ready. She followed Alex out to the lanai. The enormous screened room was breathtakingly beautiful. A bluestone floor stretched toward an infinity pool, softly illuminated by underwater lights. Lush plants filled the air with their scent. The soft burbling of a spa in a corner of the pool merged with the hiss and boom of the surf.

Cara turned to Alex, eager to tell him how she loved this place, but he wasn't looking at her. Instead, he was busy getting the grill started. Busier than it seemed a man could be, doing something so simple.

Her heart felt leaden. She wanted to go to him and ask him what was happening. Was he sorry they'd made love?

"Alex?" she whispered.

He turned toward her, his face devoid of expression. "Is a merlot okay?"

"What?"

"To drink. I thought I'd open a bottle of merlot."

Half an hour ago, she'd have laughed and admitted she wouldn't know merlot the wine from Merlin the Magician.

But not now.

"Cara?"

"Yes," she said brightly. "Merlot sounds fine."

He went back into the house, returned with a bottle, a corkscrew and two glasses. The wine shimmered like garnets as he poured it and slipped down her throat like silk, but she had no idea what it tasted like.

The salad had no taste, either, though Alex made a point of telling her the dressing was great. She told him the steaks were wonderful.

"Then," he said, halfway into the silence that followed their brilliant attempt at conversation, "why aren't you eating?"

She looked up. "I guess I'm not as hungry as I'd thought."

He nodded. "Same here." More silence. Finally, he cleared his throat. "Why don't I clear the dishes while you make some coffee? I make the world's worst coffee or I'd volunteer to…"

His words faded away. Cara was staring at him, her eyes dark. He knew the reason; he was treating her with the deference due a stranger. And they weren't strangers, not now, not after all they'd shared. Danger. Argument. Anger. Laughter. Above all, those hours in each other's arms.

He tossed his napkin on the table and shoved back his chair. His glass went crashing to the floor. Who cared about broken glasses when he'd broken Cara's heart?

"Baby," he said, and pulled her into his arms. "Sweetheart, forgive me."

She shook her head, her silken curls tumbling like a curtain over her eyes.

"There's nothing to forgive," she said, but the tremor in her voice gave her away.

"Yes. There is." He clasped her chin, gently forced her face up to his. "I'm trying so hard here…" Damn it, that hadn't come out right! "I'm trying to stay at a professional distance," he said tightly. "Do you understand?"

"Don't say anything else, Alex. I know that I'm an—an assignment. You don't have to—"

He kissed her. Hard. Deep. His hands holding her

face so she couldn't twist away; his mouth open and demanding so she couldn't misinterpret how he felt about her. When, finally, she made a soft little sound and put her hands on his chest, he changed the kiss, made it gentle and giving and gathered her tightly in his arms.

"Yes," he said roughly, his lips a breath from hers. "You were an assignment. I was supposed to keep you safe. But how safe can I keep you when I've forgotten who I am? I'm supposed to be Alexander Knight. Operative, risk specialist—whatever you want to call me. Uncompromising. Never diverted. That's what a man in my profession has to be when he's working." His voice softened; he kissed her again, soft brushes of his mouth on hers. "And then you came along and I turned into somebody else."

Cara smiled. "I like that somebody else. Very much."

"Yeah. So do I." His mouth twisted. "But if I'm not on target, sweetheart, if I lose focus, something could get past me. Something could happen to you. And if it did, Jesus, if it did—"

She caught his face in her hands, drew it down and pressed her mouth to his.

"Nothing will happen to me, Alex. Not with you to take care of me."

A muscle knotted in his jaw. "Don't underestimate Gennaro. Just because I took care of those clowns in New York—"

She clasped his face more tightly, as if she was afraid he'd turn away. "Alex. Anthony Gennaro never threatened me."

"The hell he didn't. That was why the FBI wanted you in protective custody."

"The federal agents who came to see me insisted I

know things about—about Gennaro's business. That he'd have me killed because of it."

"Is that what you call crime? A business?"

"All right." Cara's voice rose. "He's a criminal. But I don't know anything about that part of his life. And he'd never hurt me. I know he wouldn't."

Alex's face hardened. He caught Cara's wrists and brought her arms to her side.

"Let's not talk about him, okay? Your relationship with him is in the past. Do us both a favor and leave it there."

"Damn you," she said, her voice rising with anger. "Listen to me. I wasn't his mistress. I wasn't his lover. I wasn't his girlfriend. I was the librarian he hired to catalog a collection of rare books he bought at a Sotheby's auction. He walked into my office at the university where I worked and offered me the job. I didn't know anything about the man, only that he was handing me a once-in-a-lifetime opportunity."

"As his librarian."

The scorn in Alex's voice stung, but she ignored it.

"Exactly. I worked for him. I didn't sleep with him, for God's sake! I couldn't. I wouldn't. Because—because—"

"Because?"

Cara took a shuddering breath. Too much honesty could be a dangerous thing.

"Because that wasn't what he wanted of me. Because I'm not that kind of woman. Because, until you, I'd only been with one man and that was—it was nothing like what I feel with you, like what you make me feel…."

Alex muttered an oath, pulled her into his arms and held her close. He tried to kiss her, but she turned her face away.

"If you can't accept me as who I am," she said in a shaky whisper, "if I'm going to see doubt in your eyes whenever we make love, then what happened last night, what happened today, were mistakes."

He'd had ultimatums from women before. *Tell me you love me, or it's over. Ask me to marry you, or I'm out of here.*

A man expected those, even when he always, *always*, made it clear he wasn't committing himself to anything long-term.

But he'd never had an ultimatum delivered with such quiet dignity. And he loved it. Loved the angle of Cara's chin, the pride of self in her eyes, loved—loved—

"Alex?"

He dragged his mind back from wherever it had been going.

"You're right," he said softly. "I had no right to question you or doubt you." He smiled. "I'm sorry, sweetheart. I promise, it won't happen again."

Some of the stiffness went out of her. "I'd never lie to you, Alexander. Not about anything."

He loved the way she said his name. The way she met his eyes.

"So," he said gently, "you'll answer any question I ask you? The truth, the whole truth and nothing but the truth?"

He smiled, to make sure she understood that he was teasing. After a second or two, she smiled in return.

"Uh-huh." She put her hands under his T-shirt and spread them over his chest. "What do you want to know?"

He lowered his head to hers and nibbled lightly at her mouth.

"For starters," he said softly, "how'd you come to be so beautiful? And so brave?" He smiled. "Most women would faint dead away if a stranger walked in while they were taking a shower."

Cara laughed. "You've had experience with that sort of thing before?"

"Trust me," Alex said solemnly, "I never dragged a woman out of a shower until I met you." He locked his hands at the base of her spine. "And when that punk barreled through the door…you didn't even blink."

"You were with me."

She said the words with such simple conviction that they made his heart swell.

"I'm sorry," he said softly. "Not that I was with you. Thank God I was." He kissed her gently. "I'm sorry I was so rough on you, baby."

"You were just doing your job."

"No." He cleared his throat. "I was judging you. And I had no right to do that." He hesitated. "I've seen some ugly things in this world, Cara. Men with so much blood on their hands they can never wash it away."

"Were you a soldier?"

"Yes." He hesitated. He never talked about what he thought of as his former life, except with his brothers who'd lived that life, too. "Special Forces," he said gruffly. "That's how John and I know each other. Our unit was in—it was in a place a million miles from here."

"And you saved his life?"

Damn it, why had he told her that? Only to make sure she understood she couldn't turn to John for help, but now he was stuck with an explanation. A short one, then. He didn't want to scare her and he sure as hell didn't want to talk about himself or the days he'd spent clinging to life after he went back for John…and before he got both of them out.

"It was nothing much. We'd set an explosive device in a building. We had only a few seconds to get out and John—John got shot. He went down. And—"

"And you went back for him," Cara said softly.

And got shot, like John, and captured, and spent ten days being tortured before he killed his guard and got John and himself out. No way in hell was he going to tell her that.

"Yeah," he said gruffly. "It's how we were. All of us." He cleared his throat. "After Special Forces, I was recruited by a government agency. I stayed a couple of years, left it and never looked back, Cara. Until now. Until the guy who heads it asked me to take on this assignment."

"Me," she said, her voice low.

"No," he said roughly, clasping her shoulders hard. "Not anymore. You're not an assignment, sweetheart, you're—you're…" *The most important thing in my life*, he'd almost said, but that was crazy. Hadn't they just agreed they hardly knew each other? "You're special to me." He hesitated, wanting to tell her how he felt but not wanting to hurt her again. "Cara, I spent a long time dealing with scum like Gennaro, men who kill what they can't corrupt for their own selfish motives. Maybe that's why I couldn't deal with thinking that you were part of his life. You understand?"

Cara nodded. Her face was pale, but why wouldn't it be? God, he was an idiot! This woman was his lover, this was only the second night they'd been together, and he was talking moralistic blood and gore.

"Baby. Forgive me." He gave a little laugh. "Talk about dinner conversation…."

"No. Don't apologize. I'm glad you explained. I want to know everything about you, Alex. Everything."

He smiled into her eyes. "Yeah." His voice roughened as he opened the sash of her robe. "The same here." He swept his gaze over her, felt himself harden as he did. "Have I told you how lovely you are?"

She smiled. Better still, color crept back into her face.

Gently, he kissed her throat.

"Lovely. And delicious. Here. And here," he whispered, cupping her breasts, then sucking a nipple deep into his mouth.

She gave one of those sexy little moans he loved.

"You don't need this," he said, drawing the robe from her shoulders.

"Alex..."

"Shh, sweetheart. Let me make love to you. No. Don't do anything. Just let me touch you and watch your face. I want to see what pleases you."

Everything, she thought, *everything he did.*

"Spread your legs for me," he said, his voice thick and slurred. "Yes. That's right."

She whispered his name but he didn't answer. His eyes were hot on hers; just looking at him made her tremble. Slowly, she obeyed his honeyed command. She could feel herself weeping against his palm.

"Do you like this?" he whispered.

His fingers sought out her clitoris. Stroked it. His thumb was on her nipple. Then his mouth. It was too much. His hand. His lips. He was fully dressed and she was naked, at his mercy. Naked and loving what he was doing to her. Loving the feel of his hand. Of his mouth. Loving this...

Loving him.

This stranger. This dangerous, passionate stranger....

I love you, Alexander, she thought wildly, *I love you....*

A cry tore from Cara's throat. Her legs gave way; she tumbled forward, into her lover's strong embrace.

"Shh," he whispered, and kissed her. "You're safe. You're safe, sweetheart. I have you, right here in my arms."

He lifted her, carried her to a chaise longue beside the softly lit pool and lay her down on it. Slowly, his eyes never leaving hers, he undressed, baring his beautifully sculpted body.

Cara held out her arms.

He came down to her. Covered her. Took her hand and brought it to his silk-over-steel erection. Caught his breath as she guided him to her, lifted her hips and took him deep inside.

"Alex," she said on a little sob as he began to move. "Alexander…"

Sensation coursed through her like quicksilver. Alex groaned, whispered her name and took her with him into the night-fires blazing overhead in the tropical sky.

CHAPTER NINE

WARM, sun-kissed days. Cool, star-bright nights.

And always, day or night, Alex in her arms.

What began as a nightmare had changed into a dream.

Cara turned her face up to the cerulean sky as the surf lapped her bare toes. No, not a dream. That wasn't a good choice of words because if this really was a dream, she hoped she'd never wake from it.

A man scared you so badly you thought you'd die of fright. He had a gun and an attitude and, considering what the FBI agents had said, he might have come to kill you.

Instead—instead, she thought with a little shake of the head, he turned out to be the man you'd waited for all your life.

How would she describe Alex? If she had to choose the right words, which would she select? Cara had taken the required courses in library science but her major concentration had been in English. Creative Writing, to be exact. That meant that using lots of adjectives was a no-no.

So said the intelligentsia…but then, perhaps the intelligentsia had never known Alexander Knight.

He was strong. Smart. Protective. He was beautiful, though she had the feeling he'd bristle if she ever used that word to his face because he was almost heart-stoppingly male and men weren't given to thinking of themselves as "beautiful."

But he was. His face. His body. Beautiful was the only word that described him.

On top of all that, he was fun. He could make her laugh, which was a small miracle all by itself. It was a long time—months—since she'd laughed.

She had the feeling there'd been times in his life he hadn't laughed much, either. Every now and then, when they turned on the satellite TV and caught the news, he'd see things happening in the world that would make his eyes take on a haunted look.

Cara sensed that her lover had seen more than a man should of the dark side of human nature.

That he could fly a plane had surprised her. Now, it turned out he was a sailor, too. He had a thirty-four foot sailboat. It had come with the house, he said. And, he added with a sexy grin, it was perfect. Not too big, not too small. Just right, like her.

The first time they took it out, he'd stood with his arms around her at the helm

Want to try steering? he'd said, taking his hands off the wheel. And she'd laughed and said, no, she couldn't.

She could do anything she set her mind to, he'd said.

So she'd steered the boat and learned to balance the sails and the rudder. She loved doing it—but what she loved most was anchoring offshore and making love on the teak deck, the Florida sun warm on their naked bodies.

Alex had suggested sailing to Miami Beach so he could buy her clothes to wear. And she'd said…just re-membering made her blush…she'd said that all she needed to wear was him.

The look in his eyes, what happened next, made blushing worthwhile. Besides, it was true. She had her laundered sweats and his T-shirts. What more did she need?

Not a bra under the shirts.

Not panties, either.

Why would she want them? They'd have been an impediment to Alex's hands. Oh, God, his hands. Under the soft cotton shirt. Stroking her breasts. Her belly. Cupping her, touching her, his eyes green and hot on hers…

Was it shocking that she'd turned into a woman who couldn't get enough of sex with her lover?

Sex can be dangerous, her mother had said during a talk about boys, early in Cara's teen years. *And it can be wonderful. That's why you need to wait to have sex when you're old enough to make responsible decisions.*

She hadn't understood that wise advice. Not then. When she learned the truth about her mother, she'd thought, grimly, that her mother had got half of it right. Sex, obviously, was dangerous. But wonderful?

Something that made a woman stupid wasn't wonderful at all.

Wrong.

Cara sat down on the sand and wrapped her arms around her knees.

Sex *was* wonderful, if you were with the right man. Her mother hadn't been, but she was. Alex was the right man. The only man.

Each day, each night, she fell more deeply in love with him.

What her heart ached to know was how he felt about

her. She knew it was more than physical attraction. She could tell by the way he held her after they made love. By the way he called her "baby" and "sweetheart," nicknames she knew he'd initially used with deliberate coldness, and now held all the warmth a man could put into them.

"Good morning, sweetheart."

Cara looked over her shoulder. Her lover was coming toward her. His hair was wet, drops of water glittering in the ebony silk of it like stars against the night sky. He hadn't shaved yet: there was sexy stubble on his jaw.

And he was smiling in the way he smiled only at her.

Her heart turned over.

"Good morning."

She held out her hand and he drew her to her feet and into his arms so he could give her a toothpaste-flavored kiss.

"Did I wake you?" She smiled. "I tried not to."

"My empty bed woke me." He nuzzled her throat. "Why'd you leave?"

"I don't know. I felt the sun on my face, heard the sound of the ocean…" She smiled again and leaned into him. "I can't get enough of your island. It's so beautiful."

"You're what's beautiful," he said softly. Another kiss, this time a long one. Cara could feel herself melting. It was the only word for it. She melted whenever Alex held her. "I have an idea."

"Mmm?"

"We'll have a quick breakfast. Then we'll sail to the mainland."

"But I don't need—"

"I loved your answer, baby. But I want to take you

out. Show you South Beach." He grinned. "Show you *to* South Beach. Please, Cara. Let me."

She knew he meant it. And the truth was, the thought of seeing fabled South Beach with him thrilled her.

"Of course," he said softly, "you'll have to pay a price."

His voice was husky. She could feel his swift hardening against her hip and she turned in his arms and pressed herself lightly against him.

"A price, huh?" she whispered. "I don't know about that, Alexander."

Jesus, he loved when she said his name like that. Loved when she sounded breathless, as she did now. He still couldn't get over how often he wanted her. He'd always had a healthy sexual appetite but his need for her went beyond anything he'd ever experienced.

So did her response.

"Well," he said huskily, "let's see."

Slowly, he raised her T-shirt. When it topped her breasts, instead of tugging the shirt higher, he used it to gently imprison her arms while he bent his head and took first one nipple and then the other into his mouth.

Cara murmured with pleasure and it was all he could do to keep from tumbling her onto the sand and thrusting into her. He didn't do it because waiting, drawing out the moment, would be even better.

He tossed the shirt aside. Reached for the zipper of his cutoffs. Her eyes followed his gesture.

"Let me," she whispered, replacing his hand with hers. He had to clench his jaw when she encircled his length with her fingers. "Alex? Is this for me?"

He groaned. "Witch," he said thickly.

He tugged her down to the sand with him.

By now, Cara knew this should have been a familiar dance, but it wasn't. It would never be. Each time they made love, it was different.

And wonderful.

Alex was masculinity personified. His face. His body. The way he caressed her. Today, she wanted to caress him.

When he reached for her, she shook her head and gently pushed him onto his back.

"My turn," she said softly.

His eyes turned to dark green slits.

She began with his mouth. How she loved his mouth! It was sculpted. Sensual. She told him so by tracing its outline with the tip of her tongue, absorbing his taste before taking a delicate nip of the flesh in the center of his bottom lip.

"Mmm," she whispered, cupping his jaw, dancing her fingers over the sexy, early-morning stubble, loving the deliciously rough texture of it against her skin.

Slowly, she explored his body. The strong musculature of it, the vee of dark hair across his pectorals, the silky line that led down to his tight abs and belly.

"What's this?" she said, running her finger over a bit of puckered flesh in his right shoulder.

He tensed a little under her hand. "Just a wound."

"A wound?"

He shrugged. "Things happen."

Things happen. He made it sound like nothing, but she doubted if it had been nothing. He had another scar, long and narrow, on his chest.

"And this?" He shrugged again, and Cara nodded. "Something else that happened, right?" He didn't answer and she bent her head and put her lips to the scar as if kissing it might take away whatever it was he wanted to forget.

"Will you at least tell me about this?" she asked, touching the proud eagle tattooed on his biceps.

To her delight, he blushed.

"Kid stuff. I have two brothers—did I mention that? Cam and Matt. We were pretty close, growing up. Well, we still are. Anyway, Cam was leaving for college. It was the first time we were going to be separated and getting the tattoos seemed like a good idea at the time." He smiled. "Crazy, huh?"

"No," Cara murmured. "Nice."

She pressed her mouth to the eagle. Nipped his biceps lightly with her teeth. Felt his shudder of response. But when he reached for her, she shook her head.

"Not yet."

She pushed him back against the sand. He let her do it, though she knew he could have easily overpowered her. And he lay still as she went on touching him, though she knew it cost him.

His muscles were taut under her searching hand and, after a while, his skin glittered with sweat. She bent over him, her hair tumbling around her face, and kissed her way down his torso with the delicacy of a cat.

His penis strained toward her but she didn't touch it. Instead, she went on tantalizing him as he always tantalized her, stroking, kissing, until he was groaning, until his lips were drawn back in exquisite agony.

Then, only then, she danced her fingers down his silk-and-steel length. He groaned again and she took him in her mouth, tasting the sweet-salt of him on her tongue.

"Cara," he said, his voice hot and low.

There was a world of warning in the word but she deliberately ignored it and tasted him again. He growled, tumbled her onto her back…

And thrust into her.

She cried out, felt the immediate contractions of her orgasm but even as she shuddered at its impact, Alex kept moving inside her. He was relentless, giving her everything even as he took everything from her and she felt it happening again, that glorious separation of mind from body, of body from reality, and as he threw his head back and spilled himself into her, she knew that she would never love another man.

No matter how this ended, she would belong to Alexander Knight through all eternity.

Miami Beach, South Beach, was another world.

Gorgeous women, strolling along with equally gorgeous men—though none were as beautiful as Alex. Sidewalk cafés, fantastic hotels, Ferraris and Mercedes and Lexuses.

And shops.

Oh, the shops. Gucci. Fendi. Christian Dior. Names from the world of high fashion—and higher prices.

"No," Cara said, digging in her heels when she saw the first discreet sign.

"No, what?" Alex said. He glanced at the window. "You don't like the designer?"

Didn't like him? She almost laughed. The closest she'd come to this label was the time she'd lucked out going through the racks outside a hole-in-the-wall discount store in Chinatown.

"No, I can't afford these places."

"Well, no. You can't." His tone was reasonable and, suddenly, very male. "How could you, when you don't have a wallet?" He drew her closer. "Not much chance at having a wallet nearby when a man takes you out of a shower, naked as the day you were born."

"Shh! Everyone will hear you!" Horrified, she looked around. "Don't talk about that now. Besides, even if I had my wallet, I could never—"

"Yes," he said softly, "but I can. And it would give me great pleasure to buy you something special. Okay?"

"Alex—"

"I know that tone of voice, sweetheart. Try it this way. I made reservations at what's supposed to be the most romantic place on the beach." A teasing grin angled across his lips. "I think you'd look spectacular, just the way you are, but hey, what do I know? I'm just a guy."

Cara glanced down at her sweats. Oversized and, now, overworn. Hot, too, considering that the temperature was balmy. And her shoes... John had come up with sun-bleached rubber flip flops that were a size too big.

She most definitely was not dressed for a romantic dinner or even an afternoon on South Beach, she thought, trying not to notice the *fashionistas* hurrying past them.

"Cara? Can we go inside now?"

She nodded. Clung to his hand and half-thought they wouldn't get past the door, she in her ugly sweats, Alex in his denim shorts and white T-shirt with the sleeves cut out so that every sexy muscle in his arms and that savage-looking eagle on his biceps were clearly visible.

Wrong on all counts.

Evidently, shop personnel could see right past that.

They greeted Alex the same way in each store, with respectful smiles and eager attention. She barely rated a look until he began pointing to things he thought would look good on her.

"We'll try this," he'd say to the hovering salesclerk, "and that, and that."

Suddenly, Cara began to rate smiles, too.

It was heady stuff for a woman who made her dressing-room choices by the price tag. Bewildering, too. When she said she'd never be able to choose one outfit from the stacks he'd selected, he said yes, she was right, so she'd have to leave the final decision to him.

He didn't say, *Is that all right with you*? or even, *How's that sound*? He just assumed he could tell her how things would be and she'd accept it.

The shocking part was that he was right. Her Alex wasn't a man a woman would argue with, not if she loved him, loved him, loved him...

"What are you thinking?" he said softly, and Cara, startled, blushed and said she hadn't been thinking of anything in particular. "Liar," he said, even more softly, and he put his mouth to her ear and said he'd find a way to force the truth from her when they were alone.

Eventually, they ran out of shops. Shoes, bags, dresses, trousers, tops... She'd tried them all until, finally, in the very last shop Alex said "yes" to spectacular white shorts, a white silk tank top and leather sandals, and told her to put them on and leave her sweats behind.

"The lady will wear these things," he told the clerk.

Were shorts appropriate for that romantic little restaurant on the beach? They had to be, or Alex wouldn't have picked them.

Cara started toward the dressing room, then turned back. Alex raised his eyebrows.

She went to him. "Underwear," she mouthed.

He raised his eyebrows. She glanced at the hovering clerk and went up on her toes. "I need, you know, a bra. Panties," she whispered, coloring a little.

"You don't," he said, so huskily that she wanted to drag him into the privacy of the dressing room. "It's okay. I asked the salesclerk to take care of it."

"Taking care of it" turned out to mean a sheer lace bra and a matching thong. Cara put them on and then imagined Alex taking them off her, later.

Oh, yes. If this was a dream, she never wanted it to end.

The café where they had lunch overlooked the beach. The waves were high; someone at another table spotted dolphins and called out the sighting, and after they'd watched the sleek gray bodies riding the surf, Cara shook her head in mock exasperation and accused Alex of arranging the display.

"I would, if I could," he said, smiling, "just to see you laugh like that."

It was the truth. He'd have turned the world upside-down to ensure that expression on her face.

He loved her laugh. Her smiles. The way she sighed with pleasure at her *salade Niçoise* and mmm'd at the chilled *pinot grigio* he selected.

"Is that the name of the wine or the grape?" she asked him, after the first taste, and he loved that she wasn't embarrassed to admit that she didn't know the answer as much as he loved that she really was interested.

And he loved the way she'd looked each time he'd pointed at something in all those shops and added it to the growing stack of what he wanted her to wear, the little-girl-in-Toyland widening of her eyes.

Even he—who had never shopped with a woman in his entire life—even he could tell nobody had ever showered her with such extravagant gifts.

Surely, Tony G would have done so, if she'd been his mistress…and, goddammit, where had that come from? She'd told him she hadn't been Gennaro's lover and he believed her.

How could he have gotten this lucky? How could agreeing to do a job he hadn't wanted to do, for an agency he disliked and a director he despised, have brought such joy into his life?

"Would you care for dessert?" their waiter asked.

The dessert Alex wanted was sitting across from him but he figured saying so might not be a good idea.

"Yeah," he said, clearing his throat. "Cara?"

She chose something from the dessert menu but only, she said, if he'd share it with her. He said yes, yes he would.

Sharing what he had in mind sounded perfect.

The waiter brought coffee and a chocolate pastry that was a work of art.

"Delicious," Cara sighed.

"Absolutely delicious," Alex agreed, but his eyes were on her.

When they left the café, she took off her new sandals, he took off his mocs and they walked along the beach, holding hands, just enjoying being together. In mid-afternoon, when she drooped a little, Alex put his arm around her waist.

"Let's go back to the boat and catch a nap before supper."

But once they were on board, below deck and hidden from the world, the slow drift of the moored vessel, the closeness of their sun-warmed bodies, made a nap seem less desirable.

"I want to make love to you," Alex said softly.

"Yes," Cara said. "Oh, yes."

They undressed each other. Went into each other's arms. Made slow, slow love. Then, still in each other's arms, they curled up on the bunk and slept.

It turned out that shorts, sandals and an incredibly expensive T-shirt weren't what you wore to that romantic restaurant.

While Cara showered, Alex went on deck. By the time she stepped back in the cabin, it was overflowing with boxes. All the labels she'd seen that morning were there.

"What's all this?" she said, looking at him.

"Beats me," he said innocently. "Better open them and see."

The boxes held everything she'd tried on. Dozens of things. Clothes. Shoes. Bags. More little lacy nothings, in every possible color. There were even things she hadn't tried on or seen. A beautiful gold chain with a glittering diamond at its center. Small, elegant diamond hoops.

She was bewildered. "How could those clerks have thought you wanted all of this?"

Alex took her face in his hands. "Because I told them that I did," he said softly. "You looked beautiful in everything, sweetheart. How could I have made only one selection?"

She stared at him, eyes wide. "Alex. I can't let you do this."

"Why not?"

"Because—because it's too much. Too expensive. Too—"

He kissed her, his lips slow and tender on hers. "Shh. I want to do it." His lips curved in a smile. "Besides, those places all have a no-return policy."

Cara narrowed her eyes. "They don't."

His smile became a grin. "Well, they should. Please, baby. Do this for me. It'll make me happy."

"That's a pathetic attempt at blackmail, Alexander," she said, but she smiled, put her arms around his neck and kissed him.

He was right.

The restaurant was romantic. Their candlelit table, on a deck overlooking the dark ocean, was perfect. The food was as incomparable as was the wine, though Cara couldn't have said what they ate or drank.

All she was aware of was Alex, dressed in cream linen trousers and a black, long-sleeved collarless shirt, his face candlelit. He never took his eyes off her.

A trio played soft, romantic music. The dance floor was tiny but more than big enough for the lovers to be in each other's arms.

They sailed home over the starlit sea, Cara in the curve of Alex's arm with the sigh of the wind and the whoosh of the sea for company.

Alex made the boat fast. They walked to the house, arms around each other, and shared a long, deep kiss on the wide porch. Then he swung her into his arms, his mouth still on hers, and carried her into the silent house, up the stairs to his bed.

He undressed her slowly. Kissed his way down her body. Knelt before her, gently urged her thighs apart and put his mouth to her while she dug her fingers into his hair and sobbed his name.

He lifted her in his arms again. Took her to the bed. Set her down on it and took off his clothes.

Cara reached for him. Stroked him. Cupped his velvety scrotum while she ran the tip of her tongue along the hard length of his erection.

Alex groaned. Came down beside her. Caught her hands and pinned them high above her head as he entered her.

"Alex," she whispered, "Alex…"

He kissed her. Took her to the edge of forever and kept her there until she begged for mercy.

When it ended, when he was spent and she lay trembling in his arms, Alex knew that he had found the only thing he'd ever really wanted.

The woman who completed him.

And he knew, too, that he would never let her go.

CHAPTER TEN

THE shadows on the ceiling were as delicate as lace.

Alex lay staring at them, with Cara asleep in his arms.

He smiled as he thought about their day in Miami Beach. Perfect, all of it, from her unabashed delight during their shopping spree, to making slow love in the late afternoon, to dinner and dancing at the restaurant on the beach. And then the sail home, under a sky shot with stars...

Perfect, he thought again, and pressed a kiss to her hair.

His smile faded.

But the day had reminded him that there was a world beyond their island sanctuary and that, eventually, they'd have to return to it.

He hadn't really forgotten that world, or the reason they were hiding from it. Each night, before they went to bed, he checked the perimeter of the house. The security system, the locks on the doors and windows. He'd warned John of the possibility of trouble and the ex-Special Forces soldier was on the alert for it.

Not that Alex had reason to expect trouble would follow them to *Isla de Palmas*. Nobody knew about this place and he'd made damned sure nobody followed them from New York. The pilot had filed a flight plan that had nothing to do with reality.

Still, only a fool would be complacent. Complacency led to carelessness, and carelessness led to danger.

His arm tightened around Cara. If anything happened to her…

It wouldn't. Not as long as they were here. It was what might await them in New York that had him worried. The attempted hit that night in her apartment had all kinds of bad-news implications. That Gennaro would try something so overt…

What if he hadn't been there? Only luck had put him in Cara's loft at that minute. And never mind her conviction that Gennaro wouldn't want her dead.

The attempted hit proved otherwise.

It was probably time to call Shaw and find out what plans had been made to safeguard Cara's return.

Shaw certainly kept calling him, leaving messages on his cell phone that grew more and more irate.

"Where in hell are you, Knight?" the director had demanded in the latest one. "Answer this call, damn it. Have you forgotten you're working for me?"

But I'm not working for you, Alex told himself coldly. What could Shaw do to get even? Fire him from a job he'd walked out of years ago?

He hadn't spoken with the director since the night he'd taken Cara from New York, and then he'd only left a message on Shaw's phone.

I have the package, he'd said, *and I'm taking it somewhere safe.*

He knew it was time for another call. Not because Shaw demanded it: Alex didn't give a crap about that.

What counted was that checking in would give him information he required to keep Cara safe.

Had Gennaro pulled back, after two of his goons went down, or was he still hunting Cara? When was the trial? What security plans had the feds made?

He knew, in his gut, that whatever those plans were, they wouldn't be enough. He'd definitely have to make additional ones.

Protecting an asset wasn't the same as protecting the woman you—the woman you cared about.

And stuck in the middle of all this was the single, overriding question that wouldn't go away. Why did Gennaro want Cara dead? She said she knew nothing about him or his organization.

That was the truth, wasn't it? *Wasn't it?*

God, what a lowlife he was!

Alex eased his arm from under Cara's shoulders. She murmured something in her sleep and he pressed a kiss to her forehead and slid from the bed. Wearing jeans and a sweatshirt, he went down to his study, lit a fire on the stone hearth, poured himself some Courvoisier and settled into a leather club chair.

He knew damned well his reluctance to talk with Shaw had nothing to do with his dislike of the man and everything to do with his growing feelings for Cara. He didn't want to take her back to New York a second before he had to. Take her back to reality and danger, take her away from this private world they'd created.

He took a mouthful of brandy, let its soothing heat slide down his throat. It was almost three in the morning. These had always been the worst hours of the night for him, in Special Forces and the Agency. Everything that was evil seemed to come to life just about now.

Alex took another swallow of brandy, picked up the remote control and turned on the TV. Sound muted, he surfed mindlessly through the channels, from a hair-loss pitchman to a movie older than he was to headlines of the day from a spray-painted anchor on satellite news.

He hesitated. Then he put down the remote, took his cell phone from the pocket of his jeans, flipped it open and retrieved his messages.

There were calls from his brothers.

Hey, man, still soakin' up the sun? Cam said. Matt's message was pretty much a duplicate. Alex smiled and brought up the next messages. Three of them, all from Shaw. The first two were what he expected.

Where are you? Why don't you check in? God-dammit, Knight...

Blah, blah, blah.

But the third caught his attention. *Call me, Knight. ASAP. Condition Red.*

A shot of adrenaline raced through Alex's blood. He hit the speed dial button for Shaw's private number. Shaw answered on the second ring, as brisk and alert as if it were noon instead of the freaking middle of the worst part of the night.

"Knight?"

"Shaw. What do you want?"

"It's about time you called in. What the hell do you think you're doing? Playing the Lone Ranger?"

"Get to the punch line, Shaw. Why Condition Red?"

"You still have the package?"

"Yes, damn it! Answer my question. Why Condition Red?"

"Things are moving here, Knight. There's a trace on the package. It's been tracked to Florida."

"How in hell…?"

"They haven't found the exact location but they're zeroing in."

"I'll move the pack—"

"No!" Shaw's voice was sharp. "Do not do that! I don't know who they are, or their exact location. Moving the package would be a mistake."

The director was right. Alex nodded. "Okay." He thrust his hand into his hair. "I just can't understand how they traced the package to Florida."

"Maybe the police officer at Kennedy."

"He's absolutely reliable."

"He's also missing," Shaw said brusquely. "Nobody's seen him in almost a week."

A muscle knotted in Alex's jaw. He didn't want to think about what might have happened to his old pal, what it would have taken for Gennaro's people to have forced information from him.

"I've worked up a plan," Shaw said.

"Which is?"

"Tell me your location. I'll fly in assistance."

"No. Goddammit, the feds—"

"Not the feds. Agency people. Men we can trust to do the job without ramifications."

In other words, men who believed in the cause as outlined by the Agency and who would do what they were told.

Men like he'd once been.

"Alex?"

He swung around. Cara stood just inside the doorway, wrapped in his robe. She looked small and sleep-ruffled, and his heart swelled at how infinitely precious she had become to him.

He held out his arm and she went to him and nestled within its curve.

"We're on an island," he told Shaw. "A place called *Isla de Palmas*."

"*Isla de Palmas*," Shaw repeated. "Name of the hotel?"

"It's a private island." Despite himself, Alex smiled. "Not in your computers, Shaw. I saw to that."

"Airstrip?" Shaw said coldly. "Docking facilities? What kind of security do you have?"

"There's a landing strip. No docking but there's a protected cove on the island's west coast. A small craft can get in and out with no trouble. Security's standard. Tell your men to phone me when they're a couple of hundred miles out and I'll shut it down."

"That's no good. Too last minute. Do it as soon as we end this call."

"Yeah. Okay."

"Do you have any weapons? Someone to give you a hand?"

A vague sense of unease sent cool fingers down Alex's spine. There was no time to give it more than cursory attention, but enough time to make him lie.

"No," he said, as if the few guns he'd stashed in a wall safe when he'd first bought *Isla de Palmas* didn't exist, as if a man who owed his life to him wasn't living in a cottage less than half a mile away.

"In that case, safeguard the package as best you can, Knight, until I get help to you. Should be by midmorning."

The line went dead. Alex flipped his cell phone closed.

"What's the matter?" Cara said quietly.

"Nothing." Why worry her until he had to? There was no reason to think Gennaro's men had pinpointed their location, and the cavalry wouldn't be riding to the rescue for at least four or five hours. He forced a smile and took her in his arms. "Why aren't you in bed?"

"Alex, don't treat me like a child," she said curtly. "Who was on the phone?"

He sighed. "The director of the Agency I used to work for." He hesitated. "He thinks Gennaro's men may be in Florida, looking for us."

Cara shook her head. "But why? I still don't understand it. There's no reason he'd want to—to hurt me, Alex. No reason at all."

"Maybe you should have asked the question of the pair of cowboys who tried to get to you that night in New York."

Her face paled. Alex cursed himself for sounding so cold but, damn it, how could she keep defending Tony G?

"Sweetheart. I'm sorry. I shouldn't have said that. I know you think the man's got a heart but… What?"

Cara was staring at the television set. "That man," she said softly.

Alex looked at the set. Hell, what was this? An overly coiffed reporter was interviewing Shaw. A younger Shaw, but that was who it was.

Talk about bad timing! The last thing he needed right now was Shaw taking up space in his house.

"Shaw," he said, reaching for the remote and turning up the sound.

The news was filling these empty hours of the night with old stuff. Evidently, this was a fluff piece about the workings of government bureaucracies, which was where Shaw had come from, way back when. He'd been some sort of functionary in the Department of Defense.

Why was Cara staring at the screen?

"Sweetheart? What's the matter?"

"Nothing, really. I just—" She looked at Alex. "I've seen him before. Actually, I met him."

Again, a chill moved along his spine.

"Where?"

"At the Gennaro house on the North Shore."

Alex grabbed her shoulders. "This guy? At the Gennaro place?"

"Uh-huh. It was late one night. I couldn't sleep, so I left my rooms and went downstairs to get a book from the library. This man was there, with—with Mr. Gennaro."

"Are you positive?"

Cara nodded. "They stopped talking as soon as they saw me. Mr. Gennaro introduced him as Mr. Black, said they had some business to discuss and closed his office door, but I know it's the same man. Why? Who is he?"

Alex didn't answer. Things were falling into place at frightening speed. Shaw, calling in an outsider— him—to do a job that was supposedly the province of the FBI. A missing cop at Kennedy who might have corroborated that a private jet had left the airport with a man and a woman on the same night the woman had disappeared.

Except, Alex thought grimly, he'd never mentioned his meeting with the cop at Kennedy. Not to anybody.

Certainly not to Shaw.

"Cara. Listen to me."

"What's happening, Alex? You're scaring me!"

"It's possible we're going to have visitors."

The cold determination she saw in his eyes assured her that he wasn't talking about a social visit.

"Who?"

"Gennaro's men." She began to shake her head and he thought, *What if she's right? What if it's not Gennaro's men who are out to kill her? What if—what if…*

"Cara. Sweetheart, when the FBI interviewed you… do you remember the names of the agents?"

"Giacometti and Goldberg."

"Good girl."

"They said they were from the Newark office." She made a valiant try at a smile. "I remember thinking how little I knew about the way the government operates because I'd have thought they'd be from New York, or maybe D.C."

Alex cupped her face and kissed her. Then he crossed the room, swung back a painting, opened the wall safe behind it and took out the several guns he'd secreted there. At the time he'd done it, he'd called himself a paranoid idiot.

"Alex? Are we going to need—to need guns?"

"If I'm right about what's happening…yes, baby. We are." The look on her face almost killed him but this was a time for honesty, no matter how brutal. "Have you ever used a gun, Cara?"

She shook her head. "Never."

He thought about giving her a quick firearms lesson and decided there were more immediate needs to deal with.

John, for instance.

A quick call. A terse explanation. An ex-Special Forces soldier didn't need more than that.

"I'm on my way," John said.

Alex hung up. Cara was white as a sheet but he could

see by the lift of her chin that she was prepared to stand her ground.

"Cara." She met him in the center of the room. He took her in his arms and kissed her. He didn't want to let her go, but he knew he had to. "It's going to be okay, baby," he whispered.

And hoped to God he was right.

He changed into the same black jeans and black T-shirt he'd worn the night he'd broken into her loft in Manhattan.

She dressed in jeans, sneakers and a dark shirt.

And he called Matthew.

"It's me," he said. "I've got some trouble."

His brother came alert instantly. Alex offered only the salient details. Then he gave Matt the names and home offices of the FBI agents who'd questioned Cara.

Matt called back less than ten minutes later. There was an FBI investigation of Anthony Gennaro, but Giacometti and Goldberg weren't agents. Their ID's were phony.

"I called Cam," Matt said briskly. "We're flying down."

"Good. Good." Alex cleared his throat. "Listen, man, just in case—in case things are all over by the time you guys get here…"

"We'll take care of Shaw."

Matthew's icy resolve made Alex smile. "I know you will." He paused. There was more to say but saying it wasn't easy. "You guys know what you mean to me. And—and our father. Dad. Tell him—tell him—"

"You'll tell him yourself," Matthew said gruffly.

"Yeah." Alex cleared his throat. "Damned right," he said, and ended the call.

After that, there was nothing to do but shut off the security alarms, douse the lights and wait.

John was already in the house, crouched behind a big chair in the foyer, a Glock in his hand.

Alex gave Cara a quick lesson with a handgun. Pull back the slide to rack a round into the chamber, release the safety, hold the gun with both hands, aim at the biggest part of the target, take a breath, let it out slowly as you pull back on the trigger.

"Can you do that?" he said softly.

She nodded. "I can do whatever I have to do." Her voice shook but her hands were steady and when he kissed her, he sent up a silent prayer it wouldn't come to that.

He wanted Cara to stay locked in the bedroom but she refused.

"I am not going to be separated from you, Alexander."

He considered carrying her into the room and barring the door to keep her there, but the way she looked at him, the way she said his name, told him she understood the risks and that she'd made her choice.

To be with him.

"Yeah," he said, because he didn't trust himself to say anything more. Instead, he drew her closer and knew that she was better off with him, anyway, because if whoever was coming for them got past John, got past him, he could only hope he had the strength to use his last bullet for Cara.

It would be a cleaner ending than the one she'd face otherwise.

If anyone had to do violence this night, he hoped it would only be him.

When they were ready, he took up a position behind a hall table at the top of the stairs.

Time crept by.

"Are you sure they're coming?" Cara whispered.

He was sure. Four or five hours, Shaw had said, but he'd also said the men coming for them were already in Florida. If he'd figured this right, the four or five hours was meant to lull him into a false sense of security.

The attack itself would come…

Now.

The front door cracked open. Just an inch, but it was enough. The gray light of dawn seeped in from outside.

Three crouched shadows slipped into the foyer. Giacometti and Goldberg, probably, plus a backup. For all he knew, there were other men outside. They'd come by boat, or he would have heard the engines of a plane.

Alex waited, just as he knew John was waiting. They'd planned as carefully as they could, considering they didn't know how the enemy would strike.

Silently, Alex began counting down from ten. Nine. Eight. Seven. Six…

"Throw down your weapons," he shouted, turning on his flashlight and rushing to the end of the table in the hopes of misdirecting the intruders' aim, just as John fired into the wall over their heads.

The intruders fanned out and opened fire.

There is no choice when somebody's shooting at you. You shoot back, or you die. John and he both knew that. John fired again. So did Alex.

In an instant, it was over.

Three bodies lay sprawled on the floor in the foyer.

"Oh, God, Alex…"

"Stay where you are, Cara."

"But—"

"Stay there," Alex said sharply. "John?"

"Yeah, man. I'm okay. You?"

"Fine." Alex switched the flashlight on again. He played the beam over the shapes near the door. They were stained crimson and weren't moving.

John and Alex met at the foot of the stairs. "I'll check outside," John said.

Alex nodded and turned the bodies over with his foot.

"Giacometti," a shaky voice behind him whispered.

"Cara. I told you to stay—"

"The other one is Goldberg."

The fake FBI agents. They were also the two men Alex had encountered the night he broke into Cara's apartment in Manhattan.

"I don't—I don't recognize the third man."

"I do," Alex said grimly. "It's Shaw."

The director groaned and opened his eyes at the sound of his name. Alex squatted beside him.

"Why?" he said to Shaw.

Shaw's gaze shifted to Cara. "Because—because she saw me," he whispered. "At Gennaro's place." An ugly smile twisted his lips. "I should have known better than to try to use you, Knight. I should have—"

A coughing spasm racked his body. Alex waited until it had passed.

"And these men. They work for Gennaro?"

Shaw shook his head. "Gennaro's not in on this."

Another series of deep, rattling coughs. Alex put his hand under Shaw's head and lifted it from the floor.

"But you and Gennaro were in something together. What was it?"

Shaw's lips drew back in defiance. "Go to hell, Knight."

One last, torturous gasp, and he was dead.

Alex looked at him for a long moment. Then he rose to his feet, tucked his gun into the small of his back, took out his cell phone and punched in a number he hadn't used in a very long time.

The man he'd once worked for, the prior director of the Agency, answered on the first ring.

"This is Alexander Knight," Alex said crisply. "I'm on an island off the Florida coast, a place called *Isla de Palmas*. You need to get down here ASAP. You, in person. Bring a cleanup team with you…and a couple of attorneys from the Justice Department."

To his credit, the former director asked no questions. "We'll be there."

Alex put the phone away just as John came back into the house.

"I found their boat, beached in the cove." John looked down at the bodies. "There's only these three. Nobody else."

Alex nodded. "Help's on the way. And, John? Thanks."

John grinned. "*De nada*, man. You saved my ass a long time back. I'm happy to return the favor."

"The lady and I are going to take a walk," Alex said. "Okay?"

"Sure."

Cara was pale. Alex kept his arm tightly around her as they walked along the sand. The sun was rising above the ocean, streaking the sky with crimson.

"It's over, sweetheart."

She looked up at him, her eyes filled with questions. "I don't understand. Why would those men…?"

"There really is an FBI investigation of Gennaro going on, but the men who approached you weren't agents. They worked for Shaw, who is—who was—the head of the organization I worked for."

"But I saw him in the Gennaro house."

"Exactly. Shaw and Gennaro had some kind of deal going on. Shaw was afraid you'd implicate him."

"But I didn't know who he was."

"I guess he wasn't taking any chances." Alex drew her closer. "My brothers and I'll get to the bottom of it, I promise." His tone gentled. "You were right. Gennaro wasn't trying to hurt you—but he wasn't one of the good guys, baby. I'm sorry."

Cara forced a smile. "I already knew that. I only wanted you to believe me when I told you I wasn't his—"

He silenced her with a kiss. "I do believe you." He drew her against him; she was trembling and he wanted to keep her warm and safe in his arms. "The important thing is that it's over."

Alex was wrong. Cara knew it. Now, she thought, oh, tell him now....

But he was looking at her differently, not with desire but with a tenderness that made her heart swell.

"Cara." Alex cleared his throat. "My brothers will be here soon." He clasped her shoulders, his fingers hard on her flesh. "We can fly you back to New York." He hesitated. "Or—"

"Or?" she whispered.

"Or," he said gruffly, "you can come to Dallas. With me. To be with me."

She didn't answer. Hell, he could hardly blame her. He hadn't planned what he'd just said but the thought of not being with her, of letting her go... He took a deep breath. "That is—that is, if you want to be with me."

Her smile was as brilliant as the rays of the rising sun. She rose on her toes and clasped his face between her hands.

"Yes. Oh, Alexander, yes. Yes—"

Alex crushed her mouth beneath his, took her down to the sand and told her, with his body, what he was not yet ready to tell her, or maybe even himself, with words.

He was in love with her.

CHAPTER ELEVEN

IT WAS amazing, the way living with a woman changed a man's life.

Alex wasn't foolish. He'd figured it would make for some differences. The dreaded C-word, sure. Commitment. He'd been avoiding it for years. And he still hadn't bent to it.

Not completely.

Living with a woman wasn't the kind of commitment his brothers had made. He was a long way from that step.

Being with Cara nights and weekends, knowing she'd be there when he returned home at the end of the day, falling asleep with her in his arms… That was enough for now.

But it turned out there were other things that changed when you asked a woman to move in with you. He just hadn't known what they'd be.

Now, he did.

They were having breakfast. A long, lazy Sunday morning breakfast. A late breakfast, because staying in bed and making love was always the best way to begin the day.

Now, with the newspapers spread out around them—

Cara reading something called the Style section in the Sunday *New York Times* she said she couldn't live without, he reading an article about the Cowboys in the local Dallas sports section—Alex smiled as he went through a mental list of the changes a woman made in a man's life.

It turned out women were funny about little things.

They didn't understand that leftover pizza, especially if it was pepperoni with extra cheese, was a gourmet breakfast treat and could even be enjoyed cold.

And then there were toilet seats. Women got upset if you left them up. And toothpaste tubes. You had to squeeze them from the bottom. And replace the cap.

When he mentioned the toilet thing and the toothpaste thing to his brothers, figuring they'd laugh and give him a hard time, they just exchanged sheepish looks and said yeah, well, there were certain gender-related issues guys didn't necessarily get.

The "gender-related issues" bit told him Matt and Cam had had this conversation before. They admitted it. Even worse, it turned out that Cam's wife, Leanna, and Matt's wife, Mia, had joined Cara in comparing notes on the barbarous domestic habits of the Knight brothers.

Alex had groaned in agony when he found out.

Pretend agony.

The truth was, he was thrilled that his Cara had slipped so easily into his family. His brothers said she was wonderful, his sisters-in-law adored her and his old man was putty in her hands.

And Alex had never been happier.

He loved waking up with his lover in his arms. Falling asleep with her head on his shoulder. He loved taking her to that elegant place in Turtle Creek where you had to wait a month for a reservation. Well, he never had to wait at all, but that wasn't the point. What mattered was the way she'd taken her time over the menu, conferred with the captain and then with the waiter, said such great things about the meal that the chef came out of the kitchen to introduce himself.

The next night, he took her to the barbecue joint he loved, where she dug into the ribs with her hands and licked the sauce from her fingers.

"Glorious," she'd said.

Glorious, he'd thought, but he hadn't been referring to the food.

He took her to a football game, to a rock concert and, heaven help him, to the ballet to see Leanna dance. He loved being with her, loved having her in his life...

And he loved making love to her.

Slowly, so slowly that it almost killed them both, making every caress, every kiss, every deep, sweet stroke last.

Or doing it fast, skipping the preliminaries because they were both so turned on that getting to the bedroom, even taking off their clothes, was impossible. Together, they'd tug off her panties, unzip his fly, and then he'd be inside her, hard inside her, taking her against the wall, on the kitchen counter and, one memorable night, in his car, where the low seats and console made passion mingle with soft laughter.

He'd never wanted a woman as he wanted his Cara, not just sexually but in his life. All dressed up, ready to go out and so gorgeous she made other men's jaws drop, or the way she was now, in baggy sweats with her hair pinned up and her face bare of makeup...

"What?"

Alex blinked. Cara was looking at him across the sea of newsprint, coffee cups and bagels, head tilted in question.

"Huh?"

"You were looking at me."

He grinned. "Is that against the law?"

"You know what I mean, Alexander. You had a strange expression on your face."

Why did it make him smile, when she used his full name like that?

"Did I?" He put down the paper and propped his chin on his hand. "I guess it's because I was thinking how nice it is, having you here."

Her smile softened. "Is it?"

"You know it is, sweetheart." He cleared his throat. "How about you? Are you happy?"

Happy? Cara almost laughed at the inadequacy of the word. Happy didn't come close.

She'd worried a little after saying yes, she'd live with him. She wanted to; she wanted to be with him more than she wanted her next breath, but had she spoken too quickly? He had brothers. A father. Friends who'd known him forever.

Would they like her? Would she fit in?

That last day on the island, his brothers stepped from their plane, embraced Alex with unabashed love and then looked at her, a thousand questions in their suddenly unsmiling eyes.

Her heart did a little dip. Then Alex reached for her and drew her close.

"This is Cara," he'd said.

Five minutes later, she'd felt as if she'd known Cam and Matt all her life. She had the same feeling when she met their wives. Even Avery, the Knight clan's patriarch, who looked like an older version of his sons and who, Alex had warned, could be what he called a little difficult at times, had greeted her with open arms.

"Cara," he'd said, "I'm delighted to meet you." Then he'd looked at Alex and smiled. "Aren't you glad you took my advice, son?"

"Your advice?" Alex replied, looking puzzled.

"About not forgetting your oath to the Agency. If you had, you'd never have met this lovely young woman."

Alex smiled. "Are you suggesting you had something to do with this, Father? That our conversation about doing the right thing was the task you set out for me?"

"Did I say that?" Avery asked with remarkable innocence.

Father and son grinned at each other. Then Alex cleared his throat. "I think I might have underestimated you…Dad."

The word, the way the men were smiling, brought a lump to Cara's throat.

If only she'd had a relationship like this with her father. She hadn't even known who he was, not until just a few months ago. All her life, she'd wondered about the man who'd married her mother. Who, her mother said, had died when she was a little girl.

Then, she'd learned the truth.

She'd hated her dead mother for lying to her, hated the man who'd fathered her. She was certain her reactions were the only ones possible…

Until she saw Alex and *his* father together, and saw years of hostility and misunderstandings set aside in one quick moment of open affection.

Maybe she was wrong. Maybe—

"Sweetheart?"

Cara looked across the table at Alex. His expression was that of a man expecting bad news and she realized that long moments had gone by since he'd asked her that simple, complex question.

Was she happy?

"Oh, yes," she said softly. "I'm happy, Alexander. I'm very happy."

Now, she thought. *Tell him the truth now*.

"Alex? I—I have to tell you something about— about—"

"I want you to give up that place back East and move your things out here," he said, rushing the words in a way that told her he'd been holding them back for a long time. He leaned toward her, his wonderful green eyes locked on hers. "I want to know you're really mine, baby. And that I'm yours. Is that okay?"

"Okay?" She laughed. "Oh, yes. Oh, yes, Alex…"

He looked as if the weight of the universe had fallen from his shoulders.

Seconds later, they were in each other's arms.

It was Friday night. The Knight brothers' usual time to spend together.

But Alex was reluctant.

"I don't have to go," he kept saying. "If you'd rather I didn't—"

Cara laughed. "They're your brothers. You've been getting together Friday nights since you guys were in diapers!" She put her hands on Alex's chest, raised herself on her toes and pressed a light kiss to his mouth. "Go have fun."

"You sure? You'll be okay by yourself? 'Cause, I swear, baby, I can just as easily—"

"I can find something to keep me busy for a couple of hours."

"Yeah, but really, I don't have to—"

"Yes, you do."

"But—"

"I have things to do. Female things. My nails. My hair." She took his arm and drew him gently to the door. "You don't actually want to hear me shriek when I wax my legs, do you?"

He shuddered. "God, no. But—"

"Go." Cara opened the door. "Say hi to your brothers for me. I'll check with Mia and Leanna, but tell Matthew and Cameron they're all coming for dinner Friday night."

"They are?"

"They are," she said firmly.

"Well, well…" He grinned. "You're one bossy broad, you know that, Prescott?"

"And don't you forget it," she said, grinning back.

Alex gathered her in his arms. "You're wonderful," he said softly. "Have I told you that lately?"

"Yes, but you can tell it to me again."

They smiled at each other. Then he kissed her. She kissed him back.

"I'll be home by midnight," he whispered.

"Midnight," she whispered back.

One last kiss, and she locked the door behind him.

The bar was crowded.

It always was, Friday nights, but the brothers snagged their usual table, placed their usual orders for beer and burgers and settled in to relax.

Until a few months ago, their Friday evening conversation had centered on whatever new jobs they were handling. And women. Always women.

All of that had changed.

Now, they talked about things they'd never imagined discussing. The house Cam was building on ten acres in the hills. The one Matt was building on the adjoining ten acres. The other ten right next to it that they'd asked Alex if he was interested in, a couple of months back.

"Who, me?" he'd said.

Now he was asking if those acres were still on the market.

Matt and Cam exchanged a quick look.

"Why?" Cam said. "You thinking of buying?"

"Maybe." Alex concentrated on his beer. "I mean, you guys are busy creating the Knight compound. Wouldn't it be a hell of a thing to let a stranger pick up that other piece of land?"

Matt nodded. "Yes. It surely would." Another fast look between Matt and Cam. "You wouldn't be thinking about building a house, would you?"

"Me? A house? What for? I'm happy with my place here in town."

"Well," Cam said casually, "so was I—until I got married. It didn't take long before I figured Salome and I would want some property. A house." He bit into his burger. "Kids, after a while."

"Same here," Matt said.

The two Knights looked at Alex. Alex turned red.

"I know what you guys are thinking."

"And?"

He swallowed hard. "And, you're right. I'm crazy about Cara. I want to marry her."

Matt pulled out his wallet, plucked out a twenty and handed it to Cam, who stuffed it in his pocket.

"You bet on this?" Alex said, his eyebrows rising.

"Matt said it would take a month. I said two weeks." Cam grinned. "I won. So, when's the big event?"

Alex blew out a breath. "I don't know. I didn't—I didn't ask her yet."

"He didn't ask her yet," Cam said. Matt held out his hand. Cam sighed, dug out the twenty and handed it back. "Well, what're you waiting for, man? Go home and do it."

"Yeah. But what if—what if she says—"

"She won't." Matt smiled and clapped his younger brother on the back. "We've seen how Cara looks at you," he said softly. "She loves you—although we're damned if we can figure out why."

"So, I should just ask her? Straight out?"

"Straight out," Cam said. "And now." He grinned. "While you still have the courage to do it. Man, when I think back on how scared I was, asking Salome…"

"Well, with good cause," Matt said. "I mean, an ugly SOB like you—"

"Ugly? *Ugly*? Have you looked in the mirror lately, bro?"

"Give it a rest, Cameron. I always was the one with all the looks—"

Alex sighed. Got to his feet. Took out his wallet and dropped some bills on the table.

"Tonight's on me." He wasn't even sure his brothers heard him—but they had. He was only halfway to the door when Matt got him in a headlock. To his horror, both brothers planted loud kisses on his cheeks.

"This guy's gettin' married," Cam announced.

People cheered. Alex blushed.

Being the youngest Knight had never been easy.

He made the drive home in record time.

Now that he'd made up his mind, he wanted to get straight to it.

What had taken him so long? he thought as he pulled into the building's underground garage. He'd known he loved Cara for days. Weeks. Hell, he'd known it forever, maybe since he'd strong-armed her out of that shower, naked and into his arms.

Into his life.

He smiled as he took the elevator up to the penthouse.

She loved him, too. He was sure of it. The way she looked at him. The way she sighed when he kissed her. Of course, she loved him.

Of course, she'd say yes.

But he wanted this to be a romantic moment, one Cara would always remember. Why hadn't he thought ahead? Bought a ring? At least bought flowers?

Was it too late? He checked his watch. Eight-thirty. Weren't the shops still open?

He'd tell her to get dressed. That was all. No explanation. Then he'd hustle her to—where? Wasn't there a Cartier's in the Galleria Mall? A Tiffany's? He'd take her inside, ask to see diamond rings, let Cara choose one and then he'd go down on his knees, right there in front of the world, and ask her to be his wife.

The thing to do now was surprise her. She'd be doing girl things. Painting her nails or, God help him, did she really wax her legs? Those spectacular legs?

He opened the door quietly. Tiptoed through the big foyer…

Voices were coming from the den.

Alex frowned. Cara didn't know anyone in Dallas. His brothers, but he'd just left them. His father, but Avery was out of town on business. Who, then?

He thought about rushing down the hall to protect her, but he had this strange feeling… The voices were low. Forced. Cara's. And a man's.

He put his keys on the table. Told himself it was one of his friends, just dropping by—except, nobody he knew would stop by without calling first.

Quietly, he walked toward the den, his footsteps muffled by the carpet. Yes. Cara was there, with a man. The guy was middle-aged. Stocky. Dark, expensive suit and subdued tie. And yet, something about him was cheap, like an entire bottle of expensive cologne dumped over a pile of refuse.

"…needs you, Miss Prescott," Dark Suit said. "He needs you real bad."

Cara shook her head. "I'm sorry. Tell him—tell him I'm not coming back."

"You don't understand, miss. He says, if there's any chance you ever cared for him—"

"I'm not coming back," Cara repeated. Her voice quavered. "I know that hurts him, but—"

Dark Suit dug his hand into his pocket. In the hall, Alex tensed, ready to rush the guy, but what he took from his pocket wasn't a weapon.

It was a necklace. A diamond necklace, blazing with the light of a thousand suns.

He held it out. Cara stared at it.

"He sent you this."

"No," Cara whispered, her eyes locked to the fortune in diamonds blazing against her visitor's out-stretched palm.

"He wants you to have it."

"No," she said again…but Alex saw her reach out her hand, then snatch it back.

"Mr. Gennaro wants you to have it, even if you don't go to him."

"Oh, God." Tears streamed from Cara's eyes as she looked up. "Please. This isn't fair. He knows it isn't. To tempt me like this…"

The man reached for her hand. Folded it around the necklace. A sob burst from her throat.

"Mr. Gennaro asked you to think about what this necklace means, miss. To him. And to you."

Her hand trembled as she brought the diamonds to her breast. She bowed her head. The man waited…

As did Alex.

A coldness, a death worse than death, settled into the silence, seeped into his blood, into his heart.

At last, Cara nodded. "All right," she said in a whisper. "I'll go with you. But—but first, I have to—to write a note."

Alex drew himself up. "Hell, no," he said, as he strode into the room.

Cara swung toward him, her eyes wide with shock.

"No note, baby. Why bother?" His lips drew back in a parody of a smile. "You don't have to waste time on a note. I heard it all."

"Alex." Her mouth curved in a tremulous smile. "I have so much to tell you. So much I should have told you—"

"Forget it." He brushed past her, went to the teak cabinet on the far wall, took down a bottle of brandy and a glass and poured himself a healthy dollop. "There's no need."

"There is! I don't know how much you heard, but—"

"I told you, I heard it all." He brought the glass to his lips and downed the brandy in one quick swallow. "He wants you back. And you're going." He flashed another smile. "Hey, who could blame you? I got a look at that little bauble."

"Bauble?"

"The necklace. The token of the man's affection. It's one hell of an inducement."

His accusations began sinking in. Cara shook her head. "It's not like that."

"Sure it is."

"Listen to me, Alex. I can explain—"

"Don't." His voice was rough, rage heating his blood like fire. "Don't explain. Don't talk at all. I've had enough of your lies."

"Please, Alexander—"

"And do not call me that!" He moved quickly, caught her wrist and yanked her arm behind her back. She gasped and Dark Suit took a step forward. "Don't interfere in this," Alex told him quietly, "or so help me, they'll take you out of here feetfirst."

"It's all right, Joseph." Cara's voice trembled. "Really. It's okay. Please, wait for me at the elevator."

"I'll wait right outside this room," Dark Suit said coldly, his eyes never leaving Alex. "You need me, Miss Prescott, you just say the word."

Cara waited until the man Gennaro had sent stepped into the hall.

"Alex," she said, "I beg you. If you'd just let me—"

"Let you what? Lie? Tell me some sad story about

how you wish this had worked out differently?" His hand tightened on hers; her indrawn breath told him he was hurting her but he didn't give a damn. "Actually," he said, his mouth twisting, "you did me a favor when you told me to meet my brothers tonight. It was a great idea. Gave us the chance to have a long talk. A chance for me to listen to logic and come to my senses."

Tears rose in her eyes. "Don't," she whispered. "Oh, don't do this."

"Do what? Tell you we're finished? Tell you to pack your things and go back to your boyfriend?" He laughed. "I was gonna wait until Sunday night. Hell, why not enjoy the weekend?" He let go of her, gave her a little push and she stumbled back. "You saved me the trouble."

"You don't mean this, Alex. I know you don't."

"Then you know wrong, sweet stuff. I damned well do. Hey, don't look at me like that. I got carried away, is all." He grinned. "You're really something in bed, you know? Enough so you won yourself a ticket to Dallas, some nice clothes—"

She slapped him. Hard. Hard enough so his ears rang. For an instant, he almost slapped her back. But he wasn't into hitting women, no matter what the circumstances.

Besides, not even putting his fist through the wall would ease the ache in his heart.

"I hope you burn in hell, you bastard!"

Her voice was low. She was shaking and, fool that he was, he wanted to pull her into his arms and tell her—and tell her—

And tell her what?

She was nothing to him anymore. He'd been played for a fool. Now it was over.

He watched her walk from the room and move past Dark Suit, waiting like a gargoyle in the hall.

Dark Suit gave him a look that said if they had the pleasure of meeting again, things wouldn't go this easy.

"Anytime," Alex said softly. "Anytime, man."

Dark Suit grinned, cocked his finger at Alex as if his hand were a pistol, swaggered to the private elevator and followed Cara into it.

Just that quickly, Cara was out of Alex's life.

CHAPTER TWELVE

CAM, Matt and Alex were a year apart in age.

Their mother had died when they were little more than toddlers. Their father had buried himself in his work and paid attention to them only when they got into trouble, which they'd done with a frequency that was unusual, even for a trio of Texas hellions.

As small boys, they'd tested the sanity and the patience of a long line of nannies and housekeepers. When they'd hit their teens, cops, teachers and damned near everyone else in authority had gotten a taste of their growing recklessness.

All three of them had been wild and close to out of control until, one after another, they'd joined Special Forces and then the Agency.

The single constant all those years had been their love and respect for each other. As boys, they'd trusted each other with their deepest thoughts.

As men, they trusted each other with their lives.

All of which went a long way toward explaining why Cameron and Matthew were seated in their favorite booth at their favorite bar two Fridays later, preparing for what neither could bring himself to call an intervention.

They weren't into trendy terms or psychobabble, they assured each other. What they were into was finding a way to get Alex's life back together again.

If it meant cornering him, hell, if it meant putting him in a headlock while they told him he was screwing up, big time, they'd do it.

"It's an intervention," Matt said, shuddering at the word *du jour*. "We might as well admit it."

"Call it whatever bullshit you want," Cam said grimly. "I don't care. We have to do something."

"Yeah. I know. We can't let him go on like this."

Cam signaled for two more beers. "No, we can't. Hell, he's a mess! He doesn't go anywhere, except to the office. You try to have a conversation, he says 'yes,' 'no,' and, on good days, 'maybe.'"

Matt waited while the waitress put down their drinks. Then he leaned forward.

"Even the other day," he said, "when we told him we'd discovered the connection between Shaw and Gennaro. That Shaw was tied to that drug-smuggling son of a bitch in Colombia…" Matt's eyes darkened. He was the one who'd brought down the drug operation only a few months before.

"And told him that Gennaro was laundering money for Shaw—"

"That Shaw got Alex to take on this thing in hopes he'd draw us all into it and then Shaw's men could take us out—"

"Even when we told Alex all of that that," Cam said, "he hardly reacted."

"Plus, Shaw tried to kill Cara. Cara, whose name has disappeared from Alex's vocabulary."

"Salome—Leanna thinks Cara's the reason Alex is acting the way he is."

Matt nodded. "So does Mia."

"Well, women are good at these things. And it's a reasonable guess, isn't it? When Alex left here that night, he was going home to propose to her. And the next time we saw him—"

"Two days later."

"Right. Two days later, I asked him how it had gone. 'How'd what go?' he said. 'You know,' I said, 'asking Cara to marry you.' And he looked at me—"

"I know that look. I got it, too. It said I could end up being disemboweled if I wasn't careful."

"Exactly. He told me I must have misunderstood, that he'd never intended to ask her anything except to take a walk and get out of his life."

"And she must have. Mia says she hasn't spoke to her all week."

Cam nodded. Leanna hadn't, either. He waited, then gave Matt a glum look. "You believe that?"

"No. It's a load of crap."

"That's exactly the technical term I was gonna use."

The brothers exchanged smiles that quickly faded.

"It's time we inter… It's time we confronted him."

"I know. We can't let this go on. He's like a zombie."

"A zombie with attitude."

"Yeah. And… Careful. Here he comes. Not another word."

"Agreed. Not a word until the right moment."

The brothers looked up as Alex reached their table.

"Hey," Matt said brightly.

"Hey," Cam said, just as brightly.

"So, what's up?" Alex said, without any preliminaries. He shoved back his sleeve and looked at his watch. "You guys said this was important."

"Oh, we just figured it was Friday night. You know. We'd grab a beer, have something to eat—"

"Ask you what the hell went wrong between you and Cara."

Cam glared at Matt, who rolled his eyes in apology.

"So much for waiting for the right moment," Cam said, "but what's the difference? It's a good question. We're your brothers and, damn it, we deserve an answer."

Alex looked at them, laughed, turned on his heel and headed for the door. Matt and Cam shot to their feet, signaled the bartender to put their bill on their tab, and went after him.

"Keep away from me," Alex said, without breaking stride.

"Not until you answer the question."

They were on the street. Alex's body radiated tension; his face, illuminated by the sign over the bar, was hard and dangerous.

"Stop now," he said softly. "While you can."

"What's that, a threat?" Cam folded his arms. "No problem, kid. You want to take us on? Go for it."

A muscle danced in Alex's jaw. "What the hell do you want?"

"What we want," Matt said quietly, "is to help you get through whatever's killing you."

"Who says something's killing me?"

Cam sighed. "If it takes beating the crap out of you to get you to talk, hey, we'll oblige—but there has to be a better way."

Alex looked from one of his brothers to the other. What he saw in their eyes put a lump in his throat.

"You guys are crazy."

"Try worried. Much as I hate to admit it, we love you. If you think we're gonna let you go around looking as if you're all alone on the planet, *you're* the one who's crazy. Understand?"

Alex swallowed dryly. "Is that how I look?"

"Worse."

He didn't say anything. Then, slowly, his entire body seemed to sag.

"She left me," he said softly. "Cara left me."

Matt and Cam exchanged looks. Then they flanked their brother and led him back to their booth in the bar.

An hour later, most of a bottle of Jack Daniel's gone, they were still chewing on the story.

"Let's be sure we've got this right," Cam said. "You went home. A guy was there."

"Dark Suit. Gennaro's errand boy."

"He gave Cara a diamond necklace, said it was a sign of how badly Gennaro wanted her back—"

"And she went with him."

"You got it." Alex looked around for the waitress. "I want another drink."

His brothers raised their eyebrows. They'd done their share of lowering the level in the bottle of bourbon but Alex had done the most.

"Coffee," Matt said.

"To hell with coffee. I want a drink."

"Coffee," Cam said firmly, and ordered a pot of the stuff.

The coffee worked. Thirty minutes of thick black sludge, they were as sober as they were going to be that night.

"I was so sure I knew her," Alex said softly. "So sure of how she felt. I'd have bet my life she'd never been Gennaro's mistress." He gave a bitter laugh. "Hell, I pretty much *did* bet my life on it, on *Isla de Palmas*. And then a guy out of central casting shows up with a string of diamonds and buys her back for his boss."

"You're sure?" Matt said. "There's no way you could have misunderstood?"

"It's pretty hard to misunderstand a woman who looks at a necklace, looks at you and says, *Goodbye, Alexander, it's been fun*."

"She didn't say that."

Alex sighed and swallowed more coffee. "No, of course not." His mouth thinned. "She said she could explain."

"And?"

"And, you think I was interested in her lies?" He shook his head. "I just wish I'd handled it differently."

"For instance?"

"For instance, I should have pounded Dark Suit's face to a pulp." A muscle knotted in his jaw. "Better still, I should have gone to Gennaro and made him eat the freaking necklace, one diamond at a time, while Cara watched."

"Perfectly reasonable," Cam said.

Matt nodded. "Absolutely. Closure."

Cam dredged up a smile. "Mark this down in the books, gentlemen. Intervention *and* closure, all in one evening. The Knights are knee-deep in psycho-crud."

"It was what you needed, Cam," Alex said, "after you recovered from that gunshot wound."

"True."

"And you, Matthew. Remember how you went looking for Mia?"

They all remembered. They also remembered that closure for Cam and Matt had ended happily and this wouldn't, but did that really matter? Alex was right. The concept of closure was what brought peace of mind and self-respect, even if it didn't bring a joyful conclusion.

Alex sat back, his eyes narrowed as if on something only he could see.

"Gennaro's place is outside New York City. On Long Island's Gold Coast. It's probably a fortress."

Matt nodded. "Like Hamilton's estate in Colombia."

"Yeah," Cam said, "but there's always a mouse hole."

Silence fell over the table. The background sounds of music and laughter faded.

"All I'd need is fifteen minutes," Alex said softly. "Maybe twenty. Five for Gennaro." He looked past Matt and Cam. "The rest for Cara."

His brothers asked no questions. Each of them had felt what he was feeling now; each had done what was necessary to survive it.

"No problem," Matt said.

"We wouldn't need much gear." Alex leaned forward, the old excitement in his voice. "Just the usual stuff. Dark clothes. Ski masks. Rope. A couple of electronic gadgets… Hell, we have all that in the office."

Cam nodded. "When?"

A thin smile curved Alex's mouth. "How about tomorrow night?"

The Gennaro estate was located off a narrow, tree-lined road that skirted Long Island Sound.

Trees disguised the ten-foot-tall stone wall that surrounded the land and the Gothic stone mansion.

The brothers had figured right. The place was loaded with security devices. Cameras. Video feeds. Silent alarms. Nothing they hadn't dealt with before. Still, experience had taught them to work slowly and carefully.

The three of them loved this. The challenge. The rush. The danger. The adrenaline high.

It was even better for Alexander.

The kick was always there, ever since he was a kid and he'd earned his stripes getting past his old man's security system on the ranch. Entering Avery's office, finessing the multilayered devices that guarded the walk-in vault...

Tonight was all that, and more.

Cara.

Cara was all he could think about.

He wanted to see her in the setting she'd chosen. A mobster's mistress in her element. This woman he'd thought he loved. This woman who had slept in his arms, who'd smiled into his eyes and whispered lies.

No way was he letting her get away with it. She'd lied to him and now she'd pay for the transgression.

Twenty minutes, and they were inside the mansion. It was dark. Silent as a tomb. Alex found the interior alarm system. Two more minutes, and it was disconnected.

The place belonged to them.

The brothers stood still and listened. Houses spoke to you, if you gave them the chance. Floors creaked. Heating systems groaned. Toilets flushed. People made noises, too. They coughed, snored, mumbled, rolled over in bed.

Nothing made any noise here. Not for the five long minutes that they waited.

Now, they communicated with hand-gestures. Split up. Checked out the back of the house and the two wings. Met again, in the same place where they'd started. Conferred with more gestures and clipped words that were softer than whispers.

They'd found two occupants in rooms behind the kitchen. A housekeeper and a gardener. Both would get a good night's sleep and wonder, in the morning, what had left tiny pricks in their arms.

Alex pointed to the stairs. Cam and Matt nodded. Soundlessly, they made their way to the second floor, fanned out again in three directions.

Nothing, Cam mouthed when he returned.

The same, Matt indicated a couple of seconds later.

Alex was the last to show up. His brothers took one look at his face and knew.

He had found Cara.

He motioned to the stairs. His brothers were to leave. He'd meet them outside. They shook their heads in protest. He knew what they were thinking. Anything could happen.

Especially if Anthony Gennaro was with her. That was possible. He hadn't checked; the last thing he wanted was to warn Cara he was there, but he was adamant.

He intended to handle this part alone.

After a minute, his brothers nodded. Two quick embraces, and then they were gone.

He waited a couple of minutes. Then, slowly, he walked to Cara's bedroom, opened the door and slipped inside. Was Gennaro here? His muscles knotted; his heartbeat quickened. If he was, the son of a bitch would be dead. No hesitation, no second thoughts.

There was nothing civilized about Alex now.

Tonight, the elegant savagery of his mother's people ran hot in his blood.

He stood in a room where darkness was broken by ivory swaths of moonlight. Shadows lurked in the corners, lending an ominous chill to the air. The sighing of the wind through the trees outside the house added to the sense of disquiet.

The restless stirrings of the woman asleep in the big four-poster bed were a manifestation of it.

She was alone, this woman he'd thought he loved. This woman he knew. Knew, intimately.

The delicacy of her scent, a whisper of spring lilacs. The silky glide of her gold-streaked chestnut hair against his skin. The taste of her nipples, warm and sweet on his tongue.

His jaw tightened. Oh, yes. He knew her. At least, that was what he'd thought.

Long moments passed. The woman murmured in her sleep and tossed her head uneasily. Was she dreaming of him? Of what a fool she'd made of him?

All the more reason to have come here tonight.

Closure. The glib catchall of overpaid twenty-first-century shrinks who didn't have the damnedest idea of what it really meant.

Alex did. And closure was what he'd have as he took the woman in this bed, one final time.

Took her, knowing what she was. Knowing that she had used him. That everything they'd shared had been a lie.

He would wake her from her dream. Strip her naked. Pin her hands high over her head and make sure she looked into his eyes as he took her so that she could see it meant nothing to him, that having sex with her was a physical release and nothing more.

There'd been dozens of women before her and there'd be dozens after her. Nothing about her, or what they'd done in each other's arms, was memorable.

He understood that.

Now, he needed to be sure she did, too.

Alex bent over the bed. Grasped the edge of the duvet that covered her and drew it aside.

She was wearing a nightgown. Silk, probably. She liked silk. So did he. He liked the feel of it under his fingers, the way it had slid over her skin all those times he'd made love to her with his body, his hands, his mouth.

He looked down at her. She was beautiful; there was no denying that. She had a magnificent body. Long. Ripe. Made for sex.

He could see the shape of her breasts through the thin silk. Rounded like apples, tipped with pale pink nipples so responsive that he knew he had only to bend his head to her, let the tip of his tongue drift across the delicate flesh, breathe against it to draw a guttural moan of pleasure from her throat.

His gaze moved lower, to the shadow of her mons, a dark umbra visible through the silk gown. He remembered the softness of the curls there. The dark, honey-gold color. The little cries she'd made when he stroked her, parted her labia with the tips of his fingers, put his mouth against her, sought out the hidden bud that awaited him and licked it, drew it into his mouth as she arched toward him and sobbed his name.

Lies, all of it. No surprise. She was a woman who loved books and the fantasy world in them.

But he was a warrior, his very survival grounded in reality. How come he'd forgotten that?

How come his body was turning hard, just watching her? That he still wanted her enraged him.

He told himself it was normal. That it was simple biology. Part A fit into part B, and part A had a mind all its own.

Maybe. And maybe that was why he had to do this. One last encounter, especially in this bed. One last time to taste her. To bury himself deep between her silken thighs. Surely, that would burn the rage out of him.

Now, he thought, and he feathered his fingers lightly across her nipples.

"Cara."

His voice was strained. She whimpered in her sleep but she didn't awaken. He said her name again, touched her again, and her eyes flew open. He watched as they filled with terror.

Just before she could scream, he pulled off his black ski mask and let her see his face.

Her expression changed, went from terror to something he couldn't identify.

"Alex?" she whispered.

"Uh-huh. The proverbial bad penny, baby."

"But how…how did you get in?"

His smile was slow and chilling. "Did you really think a security system could keep me out?"

For the first time, she seemed to realize she was almost naked. Her face colored; she reached for the duvet but he shook his head.

"You're not going to need that."

"Alexander. I know you're angry…"

"Is that what you think I am?" His lips curved in a smile that used to strike fear in the hearts of those he'd dealt with in what he thought of as his other life. "Take off that nightgown."

"No! Alex, please! You can't—"

He bent and put his mouth against hers, kissing her savagely even as she struggled against him. Then he grasped the neckline of the flimsy nightgown and ripped it from her.

"You're wrong," he said. "I can do anything tonight, Cara. And I promise you, I will."

He kissed her again and she began to weep. Her tears were warm against his plundering mouth. Let her weep. Let her scream, he thought coldly. It wouldn't stop him.

He would take what he'd come for. What she owed him. If anyone was going to walk out of this relationship, it would be him.

Except…hell. She'd stopped fighting. Instead, she lay trembling in his arms, sobbing his name as if it were a mantra that could protect her.

"Damn you," he growled. He caught her hands and stretched her arms high over her head. "You think your tears will stop me? You think I'm dumb enough to fall for more of your lies?"

Tears streaked her face. "I never lied to you," she said brokenly.

"The hell you didn't! You let me think—you let me believe that you—that you—"

"That I loved you?" Her voice broke. "I did. I loved you with all my heart."

It was the first time she'd said those words. Even now, knowing that she'd say anything to save herself, they twisted in his belly like a knife.

"Yeah. Right." He pressed her down against the pillows, the rage a living thing inside him. "You loved me so much you went back to him. He bought you with a trinket."

"No!"

"What did I tell you, Cara? No more lies!" His hands tightened on her wrists. God, it was all he could do to keep from wrapping them around her throat. He hated her for what she'd done to him. For what she'd made him feel.

The way she'd played with him. Twisted him in so many knots he'd talked himself into thinking he'd fallen in love with her…

Except, he had. He'd loved her.

And she—she had broken his heart.

Without any warning, all his rage was gone. In its place was a black abyss and he, a man who had never feared anything, peered into its depths and feared the loss of his soul.

His hands tightened on her. "Why did you do it?" he said in a rough whisper.

"I tried to explain, Alex. You didn't want to listen."

"You wanted jewels? I'd have bought you jewels. I'd have bought you the world."

"Do you really believe that's what I wanted from you?"

He didn't answer. How much more of his heart could he expose? How could he tell her that he'd believed what she wanted from him was love?

That, despite everything, he still loved her? Would always love her, despite what she was.

He cursed softly, let go of her hands and drew up the duvet. He should have known better than to have come here tonight. Rage was a much more satisfying emotion than this bitter mix of pain and despair.

"Alex," Cara whispered. "Oh, Alex, if you'd only listened!"

Her eyes glittered with tears; her mouth trembled.

His heart turned over.

One kiss, he thought, just one. He leaned down and brushed her lips with his. She sighed and her lips parted. She said his name again and her arms wound around him.

Don't, he told himself, but it was too late. He was lost.

Slowly, he gathered her to him, holding her against his heart, kissing her deeply, reveling in her sweet, sweet taste.

"Why?" he said gruffly. "Why did you leave me, baby? Why did you go back to Gennaro? Not for that damned necklace. I know it couldn't have been for that!"

Cara buried her face against Alex's throat. Her secret had become a weight, bearing her down into a dark sea that threatened to drown her.

She took a deep breath, drew back and looked deep into her lover's eyes.

"The necklace—the necklace belonged to my mother," she said. "And Anthony Gennaro is—until his death yesterday, Anthony Gennaro *was* my father."

She told him the rest of the story while they flew back to Dallas.

They were in the private compartment of a larger jet owned by Risk Management Specialists. The Knights used it to ferry important clients, and Cam and Matt said they'd never had anyone more important on board than their brother and the woman he loved.

When they were alone, Cara told Alex everything.

One day, a man had shown up at the library where she worked. He'd introduced himself as Anthony Gennaro. He'd explained that he'd purchased a price-less lot of first editions at auction. Now, he needed someone to catalog them. He'd made inquiries and she'd been recommended as having expertise in the period from which the books dated.

Would Cara be interested?

Interested? She was thrilled. She checked with Sotheby's; everything Gennaro had told her was true.

Back then, his name meant nothing to her. She didn't read the tabloids and even if she had, she'd never have connected the well-dressed, soft-spoken man who'd offered her this once-in-a-lifetime opportunity with the hoodlum the tabloids portrayed.

Living in the home of a wealthy collector while you cataloged a collection of books or paintings was not unusual, and she moved into the suite he provided.

Gennaro invited her to take her meals with him but she felt uncomfortable with that. For the most part, she ate in her rooms. She did see him, though. He made it a point to stop by the library, to chat. And, since living under the same roof as the collection of books meant she could keep whatever hours she liked, there were times their paths crossed. He was, as he put it, a night owl.

So was she.

It was on one of those late nights that Gennaro told her the truth about why he'd sought her out.

He'd knocked on her door. Could he speak to her on a personal matter? Cara was wary; a "personal matter" could mean almost anything, but he'd been a gentleman all along and she agreed to meet him in the library.

Gennaro came straight to the point. He was, he told her, her father.

Cara didn't believe him. "My father died when I was a baby," she said.

He had proof. A marriage license for Anna Bellini and Anthony Gennaro. A copy of Cara's birth certificate. Photos of her as a baby, including a duplicate of one she also owned, of her mother holding a tiny Cara in her arms.

He told her that her mother had married him when she was eighteen. He was thirty. Handsome, successful, monied. He said he was in the carting business and she believed it.

But her mother had learned the truth. Though she still loved her husband, she gave him an ultimatum after Cara's birth.

"Become legitimate," she said, "or I'll leave you."

Gennaro had laughed and told her that was impossible. Anna was true to her word. She fled with Cara, assumed a new name and vanished, as he put it, in plain sight.

Gennaro had never stopped looking for the wife he'd loved and the daughter he'd hardly known. He hadn't found Anna but he'd found Cara, two years ago. He'd watched her from a distance, been enormously proud of her...and had waited for the right time to tell her that she was his daughter.

Cara listened to his story, but her heart was cold. She knew how hard her mother's life had been. And when she researched Anthony Gennaro's name the next day, she was horrified. Her father was one of the top unindicted criminals in the nation.

She packed her suitcase. Gennaro begged her to stay.

"I worshipped your mother," he said. "I loved you. I should have done what your mother asked."

"Yes," Cara replied. "You should have."

Gennaro pleaded for her understanding. He was not well, he said; his life was rushing past him like a leaf caught in a swift-moving stream.

She told him it was too late, and she left him. That was when the FBI agents came to see her.

"The guys who claimed they were FBI," Alex said grimly.

Cara nodded. "Yes." She smiled. "And then you showed up and turned my life upside-down. I was so happy, Alex, so crazy about you." Her smile tilted. "Until the other night, when my—my father sent one of his men to talk to me."

"Dark Suit," Alex said, his eyes narrowing. "The errand boy."

"He brought me a letter. My father wrote that he was dying. He begged me to see him one last time." Her voice broke. "He said my mother would have wanted us to make peace with each other and—and he sent me the diamonds she'd worn on their wedding day, to remind me that I was her daughter and his."

Alex took Cara's hands. "And I came along," he said gruffly, "and threw you out of my life."

"It wasn't your fault. If I'd only told you the truth…" She took a deep breath. "I wanted to tell you, but I knew how much you hated Anthony Gennaro and men like him. I was afraid—I was afraid, if I told you—"

"Cara." Alex brought her hands to his mouth. "I love you with all my heart, sweetheart. I always will. Nothing can ever change that."

Tears glittered in her eyes. "Well," she said, with a husky laugh, "that's a good thing, Alexander. That you love me, I mean. Because I absolutely adore you."

He grinned. "Yeah?"

"And I'll tell you something else, Mr. Knight." A lovely flush rose in her face. "You're going to have to make an honest woman of me."

"My God, I just love pushy broads. I mean, asking a guy to marry you before he—before he—" Alex's teasing smile faded as her words sank home. "An honest woman? Cara? Do you mean—"

"Remember the first time we made love? We didn't use anything and—" Her eyes met his. "And," she said, suddenly losing courage, "and—"

"You're pregnant?"

Cara nodded. "Yes." She hesitated. "I don't know how you feel about that, Alexander, but—"

Alex slid open the pocket door. "Hey," he yelled.

His brothers, seated up front, looked around.

"I'm having a baby!"

Cam and Matt grinned. "He's having a baby," Matt said.

"All by himself," Cam added.

"Go on. Laugh. We're having a baby, we're getting married and we're buying that land near yours and building a house. How's that for news?"

"It's great," Matt said. "Come on up here and we'll celebrate."

Alex smiled at Cara. "Later," he said softly. "Much later."

Then he slid the door closed, drew his beloved Cara into his arms and showed her how much he loved her, how much he would always love her...

And what a glorious life they were going to have together.

UNCUT

Even more passion for your reading pleasure!

Escape into a world of intense passion
and scorching romance!

You'll find the drama, the emotion, the international
settings and happy endings that you've always
loved in Presents. But we've turned up the thermostat
just a little, so that the relationships really sizzle.
Careful…they're almost too hot to handle!

**Look for some of your favorite
bestselling authors coming soon in
Presents UnCut!**

Coming in September:

Billionaire Sheikh Bandar had a brain tumor.
Before starting treatment, he would distract himself
by indulging with a woman in his bed and at his
command…. Cue Samantha Nelson….

TAKEN FOR HIS PLEASURE

by Carol Marinelli

www.eHarlequin.com   HPUC0806

HARLEQUIN *Presents*®

Royalty, revenge, seduction and intrigue in—

The Royal
House
of Illyria

A European Royal Dynasty:

THE ROYAL HOUSE OF ILLYRIA,
featuring Prince Gabriele Considine,
Grand Duke of Illyria, his brother Prince Marco
and their sister Princess Melissa.

BY ROYAL DEMAND

Robyn
Donald's
brand-new
miniseries!

Gabe Considine,
Grand Duke of Illyria,
needs revenge on
his whirlwind fiancée,
whom he believes to
have deceived him.
If Gabe has to seduce Sara
into submission, he will....

On sale August

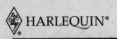
HARLEQUIN®

American ROMANCE®

IS PROUD TO PRESENT A
GUEST APPEARANCE BY

QUILL
BOOK
AWARD
WINNING
AUTHOR

NEW YORK TIMES bestselling author
DEBBIE MACOMBER

The Wyoming Kid

The story of an ex–rodeo cowboy,
a schoolteacher and their journey to the altar.

"Best-selling Macomber, with more than
100 romances and women's fiction titles
to her credit, sure has a way of pleasing readers."
—*Booklist* on *Between Friends*

**The Wyoming Kid is available from
Harlequin American Romance in July 2006.**